Sometimes Love Isn't Enough

Lurlene McDaniel

DARBY CREEK PUBLISHING

To Camille, who has been there.

Text copyright © 1984 by Lurlene McDaniel
Cover photo by Getty Images
Back cover photo by Frank Spamer, iStockphoto
Design by Kelly Rabideau

Cataloging-in-Publication

McDaniel, Lurlene.
Sometimes love isn't enough / by Lurlene McDaniel.
    p. ; cm.
ISBN-13: 978-1-58196-048-8
ISBN-10: 1-58196-048-4
Summary: Andrea is thirteen and scared. She feels her family is falling apart.
She can't even admit to herself that her parents are divorcing. They say they
love her, but she needs more than just words in her life.
1. Teenage girls—Juvenile fiction. 2. Children of divorced parents—Juvenile
fiction. [1. Teenage girls—Fiction. 2. Children of divorced parents—Fiction.]
I. Title.
PZ7.M4784172 So 2006
[Fic] dc22
OCLC: 70013559

Published by Darby Creek Publishing
7858 Industrial Parkway
Plain City, OH 43064
www.darbycreekpublishing.com

Printed in the United States of America

1 2 3 4 5 6 7 8 9 10

ONE

*T*hey were at it again. Andrea Manetti sighed deeply. She got up from a sitting position on her bed and stood quietly beside her bedroom door and listened. She could hear her parents arguing in the kitchen below. *This seems like a way of life for them*, she thought. *Arguing. All the time, arguing.* It was hard for Andrea to remember a time when they hadn't been arguing.

Her parents' voices grew louder and louder. The arguments were always about the same things—lack of money, her mother's desire to go to work, her father's insistence that she stay at home and take care of her family.

Why do they have to act like kids? Andrea wondered. She bet that her friends' parents didn't shout and scream at each other like hers did. She bet that no one else's parents called each other names like hers did. "It isn't fair!" she said to herself. "Can't they see how they are ruining our family? They don't care about anybody but themselves."

The shouting finally stopped. She braced herself for the sound she knew would come next. The back door slammed loudly. She winced. A few moments later, she heard the car's engine gunning in the driveway. Then she heard the tires screech as it pulled away. *No doubt Dad has left—again.*

Andrea sighed and quietly shut her bedroom door. She knew from past experiences that he wouldn't be back until very late. Her family wouldn't have supper together tonight. And nothing but withdrawn silence would come from her mother for the rest of the evening.

Andrea picked up the newest copy of her favorite magazine and began leafing through the pages. She had stacks and stacks of magazines in her closet. Escaping to the glamorous and wonderful world of teen actors, singers, and bands made her own world a little more bearable.

She quickly got lost in a story about how teen stars spend their free time. She barely heard the phone ring downstairs. Suddenly, Andrea's mom yelled from the foot of the stairs, "For heaven's sake, Andi! Can't you hear the stupid phone? You know it's for you. No one ever calls me!"

Andrea tossed her magazine aside, rolled off her bed, and bounded down the stairs. Her mother scowled as she handed her the phone. "Don't be too long!" she ordered. "You need to set the table for dinner."

Andrea waited until her mother had left the hallway before she spoke.

"Hello," she said.

"So, how goes it?" her best friend, Terri Chambers, asked. "Your mom sure sounds uptight."

"She's just in a rush, trying to get dinner on . . . you know. All that stuff."

"Sure," Terri said. Then she tumbled on in her usual hurry-up style. "Can you come over and spend the night? I mean, we only have about two weeks of *real* freedom left. We should make the best of it."

Andrea brightened at the invitation. She'd love to spend the night at Terri's, away from the gloom of her own house. She'd be away from the tension and frustration of the evening ahead. Besides, she loved Terri's home. She secretly envied Terri's happy lifestyle. Her parents, her older sister, Julia— even Terri's dog seemed happy and content.

"I'll ask my mom and call you back," Andrea answered.

"Bring some of your CDs and your new magazines," Terri replied.

Andrea perked up. "The new *Teen* has the best article on John McKee," Andrea gushed.

"Great!" Terri said. "We can lock ourselves in my room and read the whole thing from cover to cover."

"I'll bring my makeup, and we can practice putting it on," said Andrea. Both girls weren't allowed to wear makeup since they were only thirteen. But they did keep a secret supply of it and practiced putting it on one another.

"I could put your hair up in curls and style it," Terri suggested. "You know, a real romantic style."

"That would be fun!"

"Get off the phone—NOW!" Andrea's mom yelled from the kitchen.

"Gotta go," Andrea said quickly. "I'll call you later."

She hung up and began setting the table in the cramped, hot kitchen. Her mother stirred stew on the stove. "This will be ready in fifteen minutes. Go get Timmy," she said.

"Terri wants me to spend the night. May I?" Andrea asked cautiously.

"Good grief," her mom said crossly. "You two are already like Siamese twins."

"But, Mom," Andrea pleaded, "school starts in two weeks. We don't even know if we'll be in the same classes together."

"So what's the big deal?" her mom asked, scowling.

"We've been in the same classes since second grade," Andrea said. "In two weeks, we'll be going to Jefferson Junior High along with about half the town. More than seven hundred kids will go there! I'll be riding the bus to school. Seventh grade is going to be different, Mom. I may not even see Terri except on the bus!"

"I don't want to discuss this now," her mom said curtly. "Just go get Timmy."

"But can I spend the night? Please?" Andrea begged.

"Oh, I don't care!" her mom said sourly. "What's another night alone at home with just the TV?"

"Thanks, Mom," Andrea called as she hurried up the stairs to her brother's room.

Andrea knocked softly on Timmy's door. "It's me, Timmy. I'm coming in," she said. Then she opened his door and went inside.

Six-year-old Timmy was sitting in the middle of the floor, clutching his stuffed teddy bear and rocking back and forth, crooning to himself. Andrea dropped down next to him and took his face in both her hands. She looked into his staring blue eyes. "Hi, fella," she said softly. "It's me, Andi."

"Andi . . . Andi . . . ," he cooed to her. Timmy was such a beautiful child. She still found it hard to believe that her brother was mentally retarded. He was six-years-old, but had the mental age of a three-year-old. According to his doctors, he'd never be mentally older than eight.

Andrea remembered when Timmy was two-years-old. That's when the doctors told her parents about Timmy. At two, he still hadn't walked or talked. The diagnosis was devastating: "Birth defect . . . moderately retarded since birth."

It had been very hard on her parents, especially her father. Andrea often wondered if that had been the beginning of all her parents' troubles.

Her mother had worked tirelessly with Timmy over the years. There had been hours and hours of special therapy. Andrea had helped, too. Even though she'd only been eight, she and her mother had spent hours teaching Timmy to crawl. In six months, Timmy was crawling. In another six months, he was walking. When he was four, he started attending a special school. The school helped him a lot. Now he could recognize colors and pictures of certain objects.

"Andi . . . Andi . . . ," he echoed.

She looked him in the eye. "Supper," she said slowly. "Time for supper. Eat."

"Timmy eat," he said, beaming.

"Yes," Andrea said, taking his small hands in hers and helping him to his feet. "Time for supper," she said.

Terri was one of her few friends who understood about Timmy. Andrea had been very careful about mentioning him to people. There were always so many questions she couldn't answer. Now that she was starting junior high school, she wanted to keep Timmy even more of a secret. *How could anyone understand?* she wondered.

What a life, she thought. *I have a mentally re-tarded brother and parents who are always at each other's throats.*

Andrea was suddenly very glad that she was spending the night at Terri's. She needed a quiet night away from home with just her magazines, her makeup, and her best friend.

TWO

"So what do you think? Is the world ready for the new Andrea Manetti?" Andrea asked. She sat in front of Terri's bedroom mirror and looked at herself.

She'd taken off for Terri's house as soon as she'd finished the supper dishes. Her mother had been in a rotten mood, and Andrea couldn't wait to leave. After she had greeted Terri's folks, both girls had hurried up to Terri's room and had begun their makeup session. Now, an hour later, they sat surveying the results.

Andrea's light brown hair was piled high on her head in a mass of loose curls. Her face was artfully covered with makeup—pale pink lipstick, shimmering gold eye shadow, and strokes of rose blush. Terri stared at her friend's image for a few minutes. She tilted her head to one side and put down the can of hair spray she was holding.

"I don't know," she mused. "Do you think we overdid it?"

They both picked up the magazine and compared the face of a teen star with the one they had created for Andrea. It was close, but something was missing. "Experience," Andrea finally said. "That's what's missing. I don't look like I have any experience at being a star."

"Hmmm . . . ," Terri said. "Maybe so. But you do look kind of sexy."

Andrea stared hard into the mirror and saw the look of admiration on Terri's face.

"I could never look like you do. Every time I put this stuff on, I look like I'm going to a costume party," Terri confessed.

"Don't be silly," Andrea told her. But secretly she was pleased that Terri was envious of her.

"Let's try some clothes on to fit my image," Andrea suggested. The two girls rummaged through Terri's closet and eventually settled on a pair of flared jeans and an embroidered tank top. Wooden platform sandals completed the outfit.

"You look good," Terri said.

Andrea liked what she saw in the mirror, too. "It's not too bad," she said. Andrea giggled. "When I'm a big recording star, I'll tell the world that Terri Chambers helped create my image."

"I'll bet you will be, too," Terri said.

"Will be what?" Andrea asked, puckering her mouth and leaning in closer to the mirror.

"A big singing star," Terri said. "Why don't we put on my new CD? I think you sound just like the lead singer when you sing along."

Andrea smiled to herself. Next to makeup, movies, and magazines, her passion was singing. She'd been blessed with a powerful, rich voice that made her sound older than her thirteen years. She'd been singing since she was five, and everyone had always told her the same thing. "With a voice like that, you ought to be a star!"

So, Andrea had decided that that was *exactly* what she was going to be someday—a big recording star. She'd been singing in her church choir for years and was in all the talent shows, plays, and concerts throughout elementary school. "You know," Andrea told Terri. "The main thing I'm looking forward to at Jefferson is that I can take chorus. I'm going to try out for their show choir, too."

"Paula Winski says that show choir is hard for a seventh grader to make," Terri warned.

"So what does Paula know?" Andrea said with a shrug. "I've been beating her out of singing parts for years. She's probably just making it sound hard."

"Hey, I'm on *your* side," Terri said. "I think you can make it in a heartbeat."

"What do you think it's going to be like?" Andrea asked, throwing herself across Terri's bed.

"Junior high?" Terri asked as she sorted through the CDs. "Different—my mom says she had a blast in junior high and high school."

"Your mother would have fun anyplace," Andrea said, thinking about her own short-tempered mother.

"That's true. But no matter what happens at school this year, no matter how much we get separated, you'll always be my best friend," Terri said.

Andrea smiled at her. "You'll always be my best friend, too."

"Think there will be any cute guys?" Terri asked.

"Have to be," Andrea said. "The Law of Averages says that in a school with seven hundred kids, there HAVE to be *some* cute guys."

"I hope so. If I have to look at creepy Bradley Johnson one more year . . ." Terri's threat trailed off.

"Well, we won't sweat it now," Andrea said with a sigh. Then she added, "I think you'd better get out the makeup remover. I have to get this junk off my face before it turns into zit city."

"Yeah," Terri said with a laugh. "We can't have tomorrow's big star turn up with a face full of pimples."

Terri slipped a CD into her stereo. Then they started cleansing Andrea's face.

🐾 🐾 🐾 🐾 🐾 🐾 🐾

"Julia, do you have to read at the breakfast table?" Mrs. Chambers asked her older daughter as she poured orange juice for everyone.

"Ah, Mom," eighteen-year-old Julia complained. "Classes start next week at the junior college. I need to figure out my schedule."

"Your mother's right, Julia," Mr. Chambers interjected softly. "The breakfast table is no place for reading. Besides, Terri's got Andrea here. We don't want to be rude."

Andrea gave Julia an apologetic smile and took a gulp of the freshly squeezed juice. She bet that her own mom wasn't even out of bed yet, much less fixing breakfast for Timmy. Guiltily, she remembered her brother. *Bet he's parked in front of the TV*, she thought.

"Here's breakfast," Terri's mom said, setting a heaping platter of steaming hotcakes and bacon down on the table. "Dig in. There's plenty."

"Mom . . . ," Julia began. "These things have a million calories in them!"

"Calories, smalories," Mrs. Chambers said with a chuckle. "You're growing girls. You need to keep up your strength."

Julia sighed and made a big production of taking one pancake, one piece of bacon, and one brief drizzle of syrup. Andrea helped herself to three pancakes and three pieces of bacon and then drowned her plate in syrup. She'd eaten Mrs. Chambers' pancakes before, and they were delicious.

"Tell me, Andrea, how does your father like his new job?" Mr. Chambers asked between bites.

"All right, I guess. But he travels a lot," Andrea answered.

She didn't want to hint about her unhappy home life since a lot of her parents' problems seemed to center around money and work. Her dad had worked for the factory downtown for fifteen years. So had half the town. Then last year, the factory suddenly shut down. Hundreds of men and women were laid off from their jobs, her dad included. He'd worked his way up over the years and was one of the company's best workers. It didn't matter—he was laid off just like everybody else.

After months of searching for work, he finally landed a job as a salesman. Andrea knew he hated the job. He hated being away from home so much, but there was nothing he could do about it. And lately, whenever he *was* home, he and her mom did nothing but fight. They fought about money. They fought about work. They fought about everything. It had been a tough year for all of them.

Terri's dad was one of the few men in the neighborhood who didn't work for the factory, so he was one of the lucky few who was unaffected by the shutdown. Andrea envied Terri for that. She knew Terri had no idea what it was like to hear parents yelling at each other all the time. And Andrea didn't want her to know, either. Some things she couldn't share, not even with her best friend.

"Your dad's a good worker," Mr. Chambers continued. "Sales jobs can be hard in the beginning. But he'll do all right. I'll bet on that."

"Yeah," Andrea said and smiled weakly. She wished he would change the subject.

"Andrea, would your mother let you come shopping with Terri and me this morning?" Mrs. Chambers interrupted. "School's about to start, and Terri needs some new clothes."

"I'll call her and ask," Andrea said. Of course, she'd love to go! Shopping with Terri and her mom was always a lot of fun. Standing by and watching Terri get new outfits for school would be hard, because Andrea knew that she'd have to make do with last year's clothes. Money was too tight at her house to even think about getting anything new for school.

"Good!" Mrs. Chambers said cheerily. "You call her and ask, and I'll get the table cleared off. Maybe we can have lunch downtown at Ringold's."

Andrea hoped so. It was the best department store in town, and she'd feel pretty special eating lunch there.

She promised herself silently, *When I make it big . . . when I'm a really important star, I'll come back to this city and take Terri and her mom and even Julia to Ringegold's for lunch. I'll pay for everything, and I'll have special people to keep the crowds away.*

More than anything in the world, Andrea wanted to do that. She would buy only the finest clothes, eat in only the best places, have only the nicest friends. She'd never have to depend on some dumb factory for a job.

Just wait! she told herself fiercely. *Just wait and see!*

THREE

"Here he comes! The tickle monster is going to get you!" Jim Manetti called from his position on his hands and knees on the living room floor.

Timmy squealed with delight and hid behind the overstuffed chair. Andrea ducked behind the sofa and tried to stifle her laughter.

"Stay there, Timmy!" she called. "He can't get both of us at once."

Timmy quickly crawled to the far side of the room. The "tickle monster" grabbed him by his foot as he tried to slip past. Timmy let out peals of laughter as his father tickled him, and they rolled around on the floor together.

"I'll rescue you!" Andrea cried. Flinging a fluffy sofa pillow at her dad, she pounced on the two of them. The walls echoed with the squeals of laughter.

"What's going on in here?" Andrea's mother shouted from the doorway.

All activity stopped. The three wrestlers looked at her from their positions on the floor.

"You're making enough racket to wake the dead!" she said angrily. "Good grief, Jim! Stop acting like a kid. You're a grown man."

The fun was over. Mr. Manetti sighed and stood up heavily. "Ah, Beth. Lay off," he said. "I've been on the road for four days. I haven't seen the kids."

"So what? I've been stuck in this house the whole time!" Andrea's mom snapped. "Do you have any consideration for me?" She didn't wait for his answer. "No! This house is falling down around us. But do you do ONE thing to help out? No! You roll around on the floor playing, instead of doing the things I need done!"

Andrea's dad sighed. "I don't want to fight," he said grimly. "What do you want done?"

"The storm windows for one," she started.

"Timmy want tickle monster!" Timmy began to shout.

"Stop it!" his mother yelled. "Stop it right now!"

Timmy threw himself on the floor and started kicking and screaming.

"Andrea!" her mom barked. "Take him upstairs right now!"

Andrea jumped forward and wrapped her arms around Timmy from behind, pinning his flailing arms to his sides. "Shh," she said soothingly into his ear. "Come on up to your room. Andi will read you a story."

Timmy only wailed louder. Andrea pushed him slowly out of the living room and up the stairs. She talked soothingly to him all the way up to his room.

"Thanks a lot!" her father said angrily to his wife. Then the fight began—her parents were yelling at each other just like always.

🐜 🐜 🐜 🐜 🐜 🐜 🐜

"Well, are you ready?" Terri asked Andrea. They walked through the already-humid morning air toward the school bus stop.

"Ready as I'll ever be," Andrea said. She was nervous. She'd had butterflies in her stomach since the night before. Late August and the school year had finally arrived. This was the first day of seventh grade—the first day of a whole new world.

Andrea looked at Terri as they walked along. She looked good in her new outfit. Andrea wished she had new clothes for school. But her mother had said, "I'm sorry. If only your father would let me go out and get a job, we'd have money for extras like decent clothes," she had grumbled. So there had been no use in going shopping with Terri and her mom for anything for herself. Just one more disappointment.

"Did you bring your lunch?" Terri asked, interrupting Andrea's thoughts.

Andrea folded the bag into a smaller bundle. Her family couldn't afford for her to buy lunches either. "Uh, yeah," she said. "I didn't want to chance rotten food on the first day," she said, feeling a little guilty about not telling Terri the truth.

"Yeah, I know what you mean," Terri said.

They arrived at the crowded bus stop. The older kids, the returning eighth and ninth graders, stood off to themselves, checking out the new arrivals. Finally, the yellow bus pulled up to the curb, and everyone got on.

The bus was packed, but no one was sitting in the third seat from the front on the driver's side. Everyone passed by it and squeezed into already occupied seats.

"That's odd," Andrea said to Terri. "Wonder why no one's sitting there?"

"Don't know," Terri said, as she scanned the bus for an open seat.

"Well, then we will," Andrea said and flopped down into the seat.

The chatter increased as the bus sputtered along. At the next stop, the doors opened, and more kids flowed inside.

Andrea had been staring out the window when she felt a nudge on her shoulder and heard a voice say, "Hey! What are you doing in my seat?"

She looked up at a tall boy with dark hair and unfriendly brown eyes. He wore a thick leather jacket, blue jeans, and a leather strap around one wrist.

"I'm sitting here," Andrea said. "I didn't see your name on this seat."

"Everybody knows this is Tony Columbo's bus seat," he said menacingly. "Isn't that right?" he called to the busload of kids.

The bus had grown strangely quiet. "Sure, Tony," a few voices called out. "It's your seat."

He looked down defiantly at Andrea. She felt her cheeks grow hot.

"Maybe we should move," Terri whispered in her ear.

But now Andrea was angry. *Who does this guy think he is anyway?* she wondered. *He wants to hog a whole bus seat while everybody else squeezes into the rest of the seats.* "I'm not moving!" she said, looking Tony in the eye.

He sized her up, from the tip of her chin to her brand new notebook. Just then the impatient bus driver came to her rescue. "Sit down, Columbo!" she called irritably. "This bus doesn't move until everybody's sitting, and you know it!"

Tony glowered at Andrea. Then he shrugged and threatened, "You're just a little seventh grader, so you wouldn't know this is my seat. But now you *do* know—so don't sit here again!" Then he walked down the aisle thumping the back of each seat as he passed.

He stopped at a seat in the back of the bus, and he looked down on a trembling boy. "You!" he said loudly. "Out!"

The kid jumped up, dropping his books. Everyone laughed. Andrea felt sorry for the boy.

He reminded her of Timmy, shy and scared. Now she wished *she* had moved.

After the bus unloaded in front of the school, Andrea forgot all about Tony. She had to concentrate on finding her homeroom. A mob of kids clogged the halls. She looked at her schedule printout and decided that her homeroom was on the second floor.

"See ya this afternoon," Terri said cheerfully.

"Sure," Andrea said. She felt lost and out of place in the teeming halls. Everything was so different—so big! There were so many people. She hurried off, hoping to find her room before the tardy bell sounded.

In her homeroom, she recognized only three kids. The teacher, Mrs. Trostle, called roll and assigned seats. After the opening announcements from the PA system, the bell rang, and homeroom was over.

Andrea moved to her first period class and after that to her second, third, and fourth period classes. The morning passed quickly. *Seventh grade is definitely different!* she thought.

At lunchtime, Andrea met Terri in the cafeteria. They compared notes on their classes, the cutest guys, and the most boring teachers.

"I've got chorus during sixth period," Andrea told Terri. "I can't wait!"

"I've got math," Terri said, rolling her eyes. "I hate math," she added.

Andrea glanced at the cafeteria clock. "Gotta run. Meet you at the bus stop after school," she called as she hurried out of the cafeteria.

Andrea arrived in the music room for her last class just before the bell rang. She looked around. Chairs were set up on tiers in a semi-circle. A small stage stood in the front of the room. On it rested a music stand and a piano.

She quickly made her way to the section marked "soprano" and watched other students hurry into the room and sit down. There were more than fifty people. It was one of the few classes that seventh through ninth graders could take together. She wondered if any of them could really sing or if chorus was just an easy course.

Suddenly, a small, dark-haired woman entered the room. She walked authoritatively to the front of the room and looked around. "I'm

Ms. Vesper," she said crisply. "I'm new here at Jefferson. Mr. Stabler retired. If you're here to sing, then we'll get along fine. If you aren't, then I suggest you sign up for study hall instead. I've got plans for my students this year. Big plans."

Many of the students let out a collective groan. That answered Andrea's question. Most of the kids in the room were there because they considered chorus a do-nothing course.

Before Ms. Vesper could go on, the door opened, and Tony Columbo sauntered into the room. Andrea felt her stomach drop. *Oh, no!* she thought. *Not that creep.*

"You're late!" Ms. Vesper snapped.

Tony rolled his eyes at her.

Ms. Vesper didn't back down. "Sit!" she ordered. Everyone in the room held their breaths to see what Tony was going to do.

FOUR

Tony stared with a cold, hard sneer. Ms. Vesper stared back, her eyes boring into his. "I said, 'Sit down!'" she repeated.

Finally, Tony broke the tension in the air with a half-laugh and said condescendingly, "You're the boss." He plopped down in the front row of the baritone section. Andrea shuddered inwardly, disliking Tony all the more.

"All right," Ms. Vesper said as she turned back to the class. "How many of you are here because you really like to sing?"

Everybody looked around at each other. Finally some of the students tentatively raised their hands, including Andrea. In total, about thirty-five kids made up the group of "real" singers.

"Good!" Ms. Vesper called. "For the rest of you," she continued, "I'll give you a choice. Either plan to become interested in singing or change your schedule and take another subject during sixth period." Everyone shuffled and began to whisper. Ms. Vesper held up her hand and added, "For the students who really want to sing, I'm going to begin auditions for show choir next Monday during class.

"The show choir will have fifteen voices. Only the best of you will make it. Being in show choir will be a privilege. We'll be working hard. I've planned several community and school performances during the school year. If you think you want to try out, then sign up after class."

As Ms. Vesper talked, Andrea grew more and more excited. She wanted to make the show choir more than anything! She knew that she could sing. Now she just had to show Ms. Vesper.

The rest of class passed quickly. Ms. Vesper handed out sheet music to each section and found two girls in the class who played piano. She directed a few simple choral arrangements and listened from various places in the room to the blend and balance of the voices. Chorus was over all too soon for Andrea as the bell rang signaling the end of class.

Andrea gathered her things and headed for the bus-loading zone in front of the gym to meet Terri. They boarded their bus and were careful to sit in the back, far from Tony Columbo's "special" seat. But Tony never got on the bus, and after five minutes of loading, the bus left. Andrea was relieved. She didn't want any more run-ins Tony today.

It's a shame he is such a pain. Remembering his face, she thought he was sort of good-looking.

🐾 🐾 🐾 🐾 🐾 🐾 🐾

The house was a mess. Andrea trudged up the stairs to her room and tossed her books down on her bed with a sigh. *Why is it so hard for Mom to clean up?* she thought angrily. *What else does she do all day long?*

"Andi!" her mother called from the foot of the stairs.

"What?" Andrea answered impatiently.

"Andi, I have to go out for a while. You have to watch Timmy," her mom said.

"But I've got homework," Andrea protested.

"Do it later!" her mom snapped. "Your father just called to say he wouldn't be home tonight."

"Swell," Andrea muttered. "Another happy night at the Manettis."

"I'm sick of sitting around this house," her mother continued. "I'm going out!"

Andrea heard the door slam as her mother left.

She went down the hall and knocked on Timmy's door then opened it. He was sitting in his usual position in the middle of the floor, his legs crossed, rocking back and forth.

"Hi, bubba," she said, touching his shoulder.

Timmy focused on her face and smiled sweetly. "Andi . . . Andi . . . ," he echoed.

She suddenly felt like crying. Today had been her first day of school, and her mother had never even asked her about it. Her dad was off on business, and Timmy was oblivious to everything. "What a mess," she said sadly.

"Timmy clean up!" her brother said brightly, jumping to his feet and going over to his worktable. She followed him and ruffled his hair. *In a way he is lucky to not understand*, she thought. *He is in his own private world where happiness is a full stomach, a warm bed, and a fuzzy teddy bear.*

"If only life were that simple," she murmured.

The next few days passed quickly for Andrea. Her classes were interesting. She made a couple of new friends. She studied more at night and found less time for her magazines and daydreaming fantasies. Although she and Terri still walked to and from to the bus stop together and talked on the phone every night, Andrea felt distanced from her. She sensed her world was changing and becoming more complex.

She also made a conscious effort to stay out of Tony Columbo's way. When she saw him hanging around the halls, she avoided him by taking a different route—even if it took her longer to get where she was going. She had overheard two girls in the restroom say he'd been in the principal's office twice during the first week of school for skipping class. Yet he was always in chorus and, strangely, at times seemed almost interested in the class.

Of course, that was easy with Ms. Vesper in charge. Everyone who had chosen to stay in chorus seemed to like her. Despite the strict way she ran her classroom, she was full of energy. She pushed her students to work hard, but no one seemed to mind. Students liked to please her. Andrea thought Ms. Vesper was the best teacher she'd ever had in school. She wished the rest of her teachers were as interesting and passionate as the dynamic little chorus teacher.

When it came time for Andrea to audition for show choir, she was nervous. But once the music started, she sang flawlessly, and Ms. Vesper nodded her approval. "Very good, Andrea!" she said. "You have a powerful voice."

"Thank you," Andrea said, blushing.

As she turned to go back to her seat, a foot shot out in front of her. She didn't see it and tripped, falling into the laps of several guys in the first row. "Oh!" she cried.

Everyone began to laugh, and Andrea felt her face turn red. "Who tripped me?" she demanded.

"I gotcha, baby!" Brian Sanderson called, locking his arms around her.

"Let me go!" Andrea said.

"Brian!" Ms. Vesper ordered. "Cut it out."

"Yes, ma'am!" Brian said with a smirk. He loosened his hold on Andrea, and she hit the floor with a thud. The class roared. Andrea was so angry and embarrassed that she began to shake.

"That's enough!" Ms. Vesper yelled. The laughter quickly died down to just a few giggles.

"But you said, 'Let go,'" Brian said with a shrug. Andrea got up and glared at Brian. But she knew it hadn't been his fault. Someone else had tripped her. She looked behind her and saw Tony staring hard at the piano and looking innocent—*too innocent*, Andrea guessed. She wanted to throw something at him. Instead, she went back to her chair and sat down. She was still seething inside when the bell rang. But there was nothing she could do about it, nothing at all.

"I hate you, Tony," she mumbled under her breath.

🐤 🐤 🐤 🐤 🐤 🐤 🐤

"You are not going to get a job!" said Mr. Manetti to his wife.

"Why not? We need the money! We're already so far in debt we'll never get out," yelled Andrea's mother. She added, "Not to mention there's never any money for extras!"

"That's my problem! You're not working, and that's final," her dad said tensely.

Andrea lay in bed, listening to her parents yell at each other. Their fight had begun downstairs and had moved right outside her bedroom door. She pulled the covers over her head and squeezed her eyes shut.

"You have plenty to do around this house," her dad continued loudly, "if you actually cared enough to do it. When I come home, the place is always a mess. And you want to go to work!"

"Oh, yeah," Mrs. Manetti shot back. "Real challenging work—cleaning house and washing dishes. We have to scrape by because of your stupid pride."

"The kids need a full-time mother!" Andrea's dad yelled.

"Why?" she asked hotly. "Andi's old enough to let herself in after school and to even start supper for me. Timmy's in that special school, which costs an arm and a leg, I might add! He can stay at the day care there, and I can pick him up on my way home from work."

"You're not working!" he shouted.

"I AM WORKING!" she shouted back. She paused and added, "I already have a job." The silence that followed Andrea's mother's words was almost worse than the shouting.

"You what?" her dad asked in disbelief.

"I start Monday at the bank. I'm a cashier and teller," she said calmly.

"You went behind my back and got a job anyway?" her dad said.

"That's right!" Mrs. Manetti snapped. "And I'm proud of myself. It's a good job."

Andrea felt her heart pounding faster. *What is happening to my parents? Her home?* she wondered.

"Well, have fun!" her father said sarcastically. Then Andrea heard someone stomp down the stairs and slam the front door. In a few minutes, she heard a car peel out of the driveway.

Dad, she thought. Andrea was scared. Even though she'd heard her dad leave so many times after other fights only to return later, this time felt different. She didn't know when she'd see her dad again. Tears flowed down her cheeks, and she sobbed softly into her pillow.

FIVE

"Why didn't you tell me your mom was working at the bank?" Terri asked Andrea as they walked toward the school bus stop. She sounded hurt.

"What's the big deal?" Andrea asked with a shrug. "She decided that with me in junior high and Timmy in his special school that she had nothing to do during the day. So, she got a job." Andrea felt awkward. It was the truth—but not exactly the whole truth.

"Well, you could have at least told me about it," Terri said. Her tone grew agitated. They walked on in silence. "My mom was so surprised when she pulled up to the drive-in window and saw your mom there," Terri added.

"Let's just drop it, okay?" Andrea asked curtly.

"What do you do when you get home from school?" Terri probed.

"My homework," Andrea replied. "I start supper, too. Mom picks Timmy up about five-fifteen and then comes home. I help by setting the table, starting a casserole, you know, stuff like that."

Andrea secretly hated her family's new schedule. She hated coming home to an empty house. The first few days she carefully checked all the rooms to make sure no burglars were hiding in them. She called her mom at the bank to report that she was home like her mom had instructed. Then she turned on the TV really loud and bravely hummed while trying to concentrate on her homework. After a week, she got used to the schedule. But she still didn't like it.

Her dad didn't like the new schedule either. But no matter how much he complained about it, his wife refused to quit her job. At times the house seemed like a war camp to Andrea. She was torn. She was angry with her mother because she wouldn't stay at home and angry with father because he made such a big deal out of it.

The two girls boarded the school bus and rode silently amid the noise and chatter. Tony did not board the bus at his regular stop, and Andrea was relieved. She really was scared of him at times. And he made no bones about not liking her very much.

She wished they didn't have chorus together. Otherwise, it would have been a perfect class. Even though Ms. Vesper was her favorite teacher and she loved singing, Andrea was always wary that Tony had some prank up his sleeve that he was going to play on her. However, Andrea had heard Tony sing, and he was surprisingly good. His deep baritone voice carried the entire boys' section.

At school, Andrea said a quick good-bye to Terri and ran toward homeroom. She decided to stop by her locker before the tardy bell rang. She arrived, breathless, and began to fumble with her combination lock when she heard a deep voice behind her.

"Well, if it isn't 'little Ms. Stuck-up,'" he said.

Her hands froze on the lock, and her heart started pounding faster. It was Tony.

Andrea got her book out of the locker, snapped the lock shut, and slowly turned around until she stared straight into Tony's chest.

"Excuse me," she said, trying to step around him.

He placed his hands flat against the locker on either side of her shoulders. She looked up to find him grinning down at her. She hoped she didn't look as scared as she felt. The tardy bell sounded.

"I said, 'Excuse me,'" Andrea said again. "I'm late."

"So what?" he said, his face moving closer to hers. "You know," he said in a low voice as he leaned in toward one side of her face, "if you weren't so stuck-up you wouldn't be half-bad."

Her heart pounded even faster. "You miss me on the bus?" he asked as he pulled back.

"I hadn't noticed you weren't riding it," she lied.

"I take the city bus now," he said. "The school bus driver and I agreed that we weren't getting along."

"You mean she kicked you off!" Andrea blurted out, her eyes darting past him. The halls were deserted. *Great*, she thought. *Alone with the scariest guy in school.*

"I never liked riding a school bus anyway," he said with a grin.

"Would you please let me go to my class?" she asked again, a little more urgently.

He grinned wickedly at her. "Sure. Who's stopping you?" he asked. But he didn't move.

She wasn't sure if he was going to hit her or kiss her. She only knew that she wanted out of there. She quickly ducked down and tried to squeeze under his arm. But he leaned against her and pressed her back into the lockers. She felt tears of anger and fear rush to her eyes.

"Leave me alone," she said, her teeth clenched, hoping she wouldn't burst out crying.

His mouth was very close. "Sure," he said abruptly and stepped back, putting his hands in air. "See you in chorus." Then he turned and sauntered away, putting his hands in his jeans pockets.

A rush of anger and hatred overcame her. Her hands shook as she fiercely wiped away a few stray tears. "I hate you, Tony Columbo!" she said aloud in the deserted hall. "I hate you!"

🐾 🐾 🐾 🐾 🐾 🐾 🐾

Andrea saw her name posted on the bulletin board of the choral room and felt like shouting, "I made it!" She walked confidently to her seat and waited for class to begin. Meanwhile, a few of the girls congratulated her. She made show choir!

Andrea smiled broadly. *I can't wait to rush home and tell Mom and Dad.* With a start she realized that there would be no one at home to tell. Her mother would be too busy at her job to take more news than Andrea's daily "I'm home safely" call. And her father was out of town for another two days.

"It figures," she told herself. "I made show choir and who cares?" *Being thirteen isn't all it is cracked up to be,* she thought. *Everyone always talks about how being thirteen is when kids start to become grown-ups. But what's the big deal about being grown-up when grown-ups don't have time for their kids or each other? I'd be better off being a little kid again. At least I'd have someone waiting for me at home—someone to talk to!*

🐾 🐾 🐾 🐾 🐾 🐾 🐾

"Boy, am I tired!" Andrea's mother said with a big sigh as she kicked off her shoes and flopped onto the sofa. "I didn't realize tellers spent so much time on their feet," she added.

"Dinner's almost ready," Andrea said.

Mrs. Manetti leaned into the sofa and closed her eyes. "Timmy!" she yelled. "Turn down the TV!"

Timmy sat staring at the cartoon characters on the screen. But he didn't move. "I said, 'Turn it down!'" she yelled again. "Or I'll turn it off!"

Timmy began to wail and rock. But he didn't turn down the volume. Suddenly, Mrs. Manetti leaped from the sofa and seized Timmy by his arm. "You listen to me, young man!" she yelled. "Stop that crying! Do you hear me? Stop it!"

Andrea jumped forward and grabbed her brother. "I'll take him upstairs and help him wash up for dinner," she cried.

Her mother glared. Then she flopped down. "I'm sorry," she said. "I'm just wiped out. That's all."

Andrea hustled Timmy up the stairs toward the bathroom. She felt like crying along with Timmy. Her mother was angrier than ever, and she was tired all the time. *Is it going to be like this forever?* she wondered. *If the job is such a burden, why doesn't she just quit? It would certainly make Dad happy. Why is a stupid job so important anyway?*

Later that week, Andrea lay in bed staring into the dark. Her parents had been fighting again. But unlike other times, they weren't yelling. Instead, they were whispering in the hallway.

Andrea crept out of her bed and eased toward the door. It wasn't right, spying on them. She knew that. But she wanted to know what was going on between them. She opened the door a crack and sat down on the floor and listened. Their voices were low and very serious.

"I don't see any other way," her mom was saying. "This is no way to live. I want a divorce."

Divorce! The word hit Andrea like a stone. It was impossible! Her parents couldn't get a divorce.

"You've been planning this for a long time, haven't you?" Her dad's voice was low and accusing. "That's why you got that job, isn't it?"

"No." Her mom sighed heavily. "I got the job because I needed to get out. I was going crazy. I wanted to contribute and to feel I'm worth something."

"What about the kids?" he asked.

Andrea's heart froze. He was agreeing to the divorce! He wasn't even arguing about it. He wanted it, too!

"I'll keep the kids," she said. "They need as little change as possible. You're always on the road anyway. You can have all the visitation rights you want."

"Thanks," he said tersely. "So this is it. Fifteen years, and now it's over."

"It is for me," her mom said. "And if you'd just admit it, it's been over for you, too."

Andrea couldn't listen anymore. She crawled back to her bed and slid beneath the covers. She felt cold and numb. *A divorce.* Her parents were going to get a divorce. *What is really going to happen to Timmy and me?* she wondered, feeling scared.

She remembered Timmy's innocent blue eyes. *Poor Timmy*, she thought. *Poor, poor Timmy.* And then tears began to roll down her checks. It seemed her world was falling apart. And nobody cared, nobody at all.

SIX

"Andrea, would you please pass out the new music to everyone?" Ms. Vesper asked above the soft buzz of noise in the choral room.

Andrea went down to the front of the room. She picked up the stack of music folders perched on the top of the upright piano. She balanced them carefully and started toward the baritone and tenor sections. As Andrea passed by the front row, she felt a tug and then a yank on the belt loop of her jeans. She was abruptly stopped, and the stack of music folders kept on going. Papers flew everywhere as the folders cascaded to the floor in a shower of thuds and rustling. Andrea gasped and tried to break free of the hold on her belt loop. The class whooped with wild laughter.

"*What* is going on here?" Ms. Vesper demanded above the commotion.

"I-I don't know," Andrea stammered. She scrambled to pick up the papers off the floor. "I guess I just lost my balance." But she knew exactly what had happened. Tony Columbo had happened. It was his finger that had hooked her belt loop and caused her to drop all the folders. She glared at him. He smiled down at her and wiggled his fingers in a half-wave.

"Well, I think I know what happened," Ms. Vesper said grimly. "Tony, I want you to go see Mr. Grimes right now. You've disrupted this class for the last time!"

"What'd I do?" Tony asked innocently. "I didn't do anything!"

"Explain it to the assistant principal," Ms. Vesper said, writing out a hall pass and handing it to Tony. "Now go!"

Tony snatched the pass from her hand and stood defiantly for a few seconds. He shot Andrea an angry glance from the doorway and then left the room. For a moment, she felt bad that he'd been sent to the office. *But it's his own fault*, she thought as she re-stacked the folders.

After class was over, Ms. Vesper asked Andrea to stay for a few minutes. Andrea was nervous. *Why does she want to see me?* Andrea asked herself, waiting for the room to empty.

"Sit down, Andrea," the pretty, dark-haired teacher urged after they were alone in the room. There was a moment of awkward silence as the two of them sat facing each other. "Is anything wrong, Andrea?" Ms. Vesper asked sympathetically.

Andrea's heart pounded faster. "W-What do you mean?" she asked.

"You've seemed pretty withdrawn this past week. I was wondering if anything was happening to cause you to change so much. If there is anything you'd like to talk about?" Ms. Vesper's voice trailed.

Andrea dropped her gaze and stared at her hands in her lap. *Nothing much, except that my parents are talking about getting a divorce*, she thought sadly. In her head, she replayed the conversation between her parents that she had overheard. Her dad had gone out of town on business again the very next day. So the talk about divorce was on hold. But Andrea was sure her parents would bring it up soon. *How can I tell Ms. Vesper what was really wrong? How can I tell anyone?*

"Is it—is it Tony?" Ms. Vesper asked gently. "I know he harasses you a lot."

"Oh, no," Andrea said quickly. "Tony's a pain. But it's not him. It's nothing, really. Just some stuff on my mind."

"I hate to see a talented student like you not performing your best, Andrea," Ms. Vesper continued. She paused. "If it is Tony, please ignore him. I don't mean to excuse his behavior, but I think he's had some rough times. He hides behind that 'tough guy' façade, you know," she added. "He's actually a fairly bright kid. And I think he's got a good singing voice. He needs discipline, but understanding, too. Don't let him get you down."

"It's not Tony, really," Andrea reassured her. "I'll be fine. I promise." Andrea eyed the clock on the wall and jumped to her feet "I've got to be going," she said quickly. "I'll miss my bus home."

"Of course," Ms. Vesper said, smiling. "But I'm serious, Andrea," she said gently. "If you ever want to talk about anything, please let me know."

"Thank you," Andrea said, feeling a lump rise in her throat. "I will. I promise." Then she turned and left the quiet choral room and hurried down the deserted halls and out the door toward her bus.

🎵 🎵 🎵 🎵 🎵 🎵 🎵

"Do you think you could spend the night?" Terri asked as she and Andrea walked home from their bus stop in the cool air of the late

November afternoon. "We haven't spent the night together since school started," she reminded her friend.

"I don't think so," Andrea said. "My dad's coming in from a road trip tonight. I think I'd better be at home."

"Is anything wrong?" Terri asked.

"Of course not," Andrea said, forcing a smile. "I just don't think my mom will let me. That's all."

"Well, would you like to go shopping downtown tomorrow?" Terri asked. "We haven't done that in a long time either."

Andrea hated to keep telling her best friend "no." But she couldn't bring herself to tell Terri all about her parents, either. "Why don't I call you tomorrow morning after breakfast and let you know?" she offered.

Terri shrugged, hugging her books to her chest. "All right," she said. "We could eat downtown. I'll treat," she said.

Andrea smiled. "Super! I'll call you," she said with some insincerity that she was sure Terri could sense. She hurried home and quickly unlocked the front door. The house felt huge and lonely around her. She still didn't like coming home all alone.

She put her things away in her room and went into the kitchen. She read her mother's instructions for supper, started the chili, and began to set the table. Suddenly the loud ring of the phone made her jump. She quickly answered it.

"Hello," she said.

"Andi! Why didn't you call me?" her mother snapped from the other end of the line.

Andrea realized she'd been so preoccupied with her conversations with Ms. Vesper and Terri that she'd forgotten. "I-I'm sorry, Mom—" she began.

"I worry when I don't hear from you," she stressed.

"I said I was sorry," Andrea responded.

"Listen," Mrs. Manetti added. "Your father's coming home tonight. He'll be tired. Please don't make any plans for tomorrow. We want to talk to you."

Andrea's heart began to race. "About what?" she asked.

"We'll tell you tomorrow," her mom said evasively. "Just plan to stay at home. I've got to go now. I'll be home around five-thirty. Bye."

As Andrea hung up the phone, her hand was shaking. "I know what it's about," she said aloud. "I overheard you and Dad talking. You're going to get a divorce . . ." her words vanished into the air. Once again, she felt scared and very much alone.

❧ ❧ ❧ ❧ ❧ ❧ ❧

Andrea and her parents sat at the table in the warm kitchen. Outside, the cold, gray morning blew dead, dried leaves against the house. The sound of Saturday morning cartoons came from the living room where Timmy sat in front of the TV set. Andrea sat rigid in her chair, trying not to let the impact of her father's words make her cry.

"We're telling you, Andi," he said softly. "And maybe you can help Timmy understand why I'm moving out."

They were getting a divorce. It was decided. No more pretend. It was a fact. Andrea tried to blink back her tears. She had hoped that it wouldn't really happen. Now, there was no hope.

"I want you and Timmy to stay with me," her mom added. "That way nothing much will change for you two. You'll still have your friends, school, house . . ."

Funny, Andrea thought. *It's funny how all this time they were arguing so loudly over the smallest things, but when it comes down to breaking up our family, they both act so calm.*

"Why?" Andrea asked, holding back her tears. "Why can't we still live together?"

Her parents exchanged glances. "We explained that, sweetheart," her dad said patiently. "It's best this way."

"Best for you, you mean," Andrea said, her voice cracking.

He sighed and leaned back in his chair.

"Best for all of us," her mom said softly.

"Whose fault is it?" Andrea asked as she stared past her parents at the window behind them.

"Fault?" Mrs. Manetti asked. "It–it's no one's fault."

"Then if no one's to blame, why do we have to do it?" Andrea quickly shifted her gaze toward her mother's eyes.

"Because we just have to!" her mom cried, getting to her feet. "Things will remain as normal as possible around here," she said as she began to pace.

Except that I won't have a dad, Andrea thought angrily.

"Look," her dad said suddenly. "This is too much. I've got to go pack. The sooner I get out, the better."

He rose and left the kitchen. Andrea started after him. "Honey," her mother began.

"Leave me alone!" Andrea cried. "You finally got your job. You don't need Dad or me or Timmy." Andrea ran from the room and up the stairs after her dad. She burst into his bedroom. His suitcase was open on the bed, and he was loading the contents of his dresser into it.

"Oh, Daddy!" Andrea broke into sobs and threw her arms around him. "Don't go! Please! Please, don't go!" she sobbed.

He held her tightly while she cried. Then he gently pushed her away, grabbed a tissue from the dresser, and offered it to Andrea. "Andi, honey, this is really hard for me, too, but I have to go."

"But I love you!" she cried. "Where will you be? When will I see you? I don't want you to go!"

"I love you, too, Andi. I really do," her dad said, smiling at her with a heartbroken look in his eyes.

"Then if you love me, you won't leave me," she gasped between sobs.

"I'll see you often," he promised. "I'm getting an apartment. You can come and visit whenever you want."

"Mom's making you leave, isn't she?" Andi demanded, her eyes red and swollen.

"Now you stop that, Andi," her dad said sternly. "It's not your mother's fault. We agreed on this together. Your mom and I just aren't working out."

He pulled her close again. Andrea didn't want to let go. After a minute, he sat her firmly on the bed and finished packing his bags. When he was through, he hoisted his luggage and started down the stairs. Mrs. Manetti stood at the bottom.

"I'll get the rest of my stuff later—when the kids aren't here," he told her in a low voice.

Andrea watched from the top of the stairs, trying to stop crying.

"Daddy go bye?" Timmy called happily from the living room as his dad stopped to kiss his cheek.

"Daddy go bye," Mr. Manetti repeated softly.

Andrea watched through tear-filled eyes as her dad walked through the front door and into the bitter, cold November day.

SEVEN

Somehow, Andrea made it through the next few weeks. At times she felt as if she were living in a bad dream. She wished she could wake up and find everything had been imaginary. Even when her dad called and gave her his new address and phone number, the divorce still didn't seem real.

But it was real. She was angry with her mother and went out of her way to be mean and sassy to her. Fortunately, her mom seemed to understand. She didn't hassle Andrea about anything for the first few days after her dad had moved out. Andrea spent a lot of time alone in her room reading magazines, getting lost in the pretty-picture world of other places and other lives.

One article in particular caught her attention. It was about a celebrity couple who separated, lived apart for a month, and then decided that they really belonged back together. A small hope began to grow within her that maybe the same thing would happen to her parents. Maybe after some time apart, they would decide they missed each other, and her dad would move back home.

The thought made her happier. So she pretended that her dad was just away on business and that he would be back home in a few weeks. That's what she told Terri, too. Holding onto hope, Andrea felt better and began to concentrate on school and chorus again. Her life took on the familiar routine of homework, long phone calls to Terri, and household chores to help her working mom.

"Let's go Christmas shopping!" Terri said one morning on the phone. It was the third week of December, and school was out for the holidays. Winter's chill had settled in, and festive decorations appeared in all the stores and along the downtown streets.

Christmas! Andrea's heart sank at the thought. This would be her first Christmas without her father at home. She forced the sad thought aside. "Sure!" she said. "Mom's working, and Timmy's still in school. I haven't gotten a thing for anybody yet."

Just that morning, her mom had given her fifty dollars for her Christmas shopping. Andrea had been surprised.

"I didn't think we had money for Christmas," she had said.

"I've been putting some aside," her mom told her. "I know it's been hard not to have the things your friends have. I've done some shopping on my lunch hours. You go do some for Timmy, your dad, and your friends," she'd added quickly. "Have fun."

Andrea hadn't known what to say *Fifty dollars!* It was all for her to spend on Christmas gifts.

The two girls caught the city bus and headed toward the bustling streets of downtown. Christmas carols and holiday music greeted them as they got off at their stop. Salvation Army bell ringers stood on corners around their fat, red collection pots. Tinsel and lights glittered and flickered in the otherwise cold, gray morning.

They went into Rinegold's Department Store. Inside was a glittering version of the North Pole. White doves and bells hung from the ceiling. Piles of sparkling puffs of cotton snow lay on the countertops and underneath an enormous Christmas tree in the center of the store, which blazed with lights and red and green ribbons.

"Well, well, well, if it isn't Santa's little helper." Andrea turned at the sound of the familiar voice and found herself looking up at Tony Columbo. Her stomach flip-flopped. *Why did he have to show up and spoil my shopping spree?* She rolled her eyes at him and started to walk away.

He caught her arm. "Hold on, Miss Stuck-up," he said. "Out shopping for my present? How sweet."

"Let go of me," she ordered. She was less afraid of him out in the crowd of Christmas shoppers. He didn't look so tough in the festive surroundings of Rinegold's.

"Yeah, Tony," Terri said. "Leave us alone."

Tony stared at Andrea, then dropped her arm.

"Look," Tony said contritely. "Actually I just thought maybe you could help me pick out some perfume for my mom. This stuff all smells the same to me."

Andrea was both surprised and touched. Ms. Vesper's words about Tony's rough past came back to her. She shrugged. "Sure. We could do that. Couldn't we, Terri?"

Terri looked at her like she'd gone nuts. "Okay," she said apprehensively.

The trio headed to the cosmetics counter and began sniffing samples. When Tony turned his back to the girls for a moment, Terri looked at Andrea and motioned toward Tony with her eyes. Andrea just shrugged and gave her a weak smile.

"Phew!" Tony said after about five minutes. "It smells like a fruitcake around here."

"Maybe your mom would like a scarf," Andrea suggested.

"Yeah. Maybe," Tony said.

The three of them went over to the counter that held a display of colorful scarves. "How about this one?" Andrea asked, tossing a long silky one around her neck and posing against the counter.

"Looks like a dog collar," Tony mumbled.

They all laughed. Andrea tried on another. Then each of them put on a scarf and posed in front of the mirror, Tony in the middle, Andrea and Terri on either of his arms.

"I look like a gangster," he said, making a face. Pretty soon they were all pretending to be different characters with various scarves, hats, and sunglasses from the surrounding displays.

After some discussion mixed with giggles, Tony finally settled on a camel-colored wool scarf with fringe. "It looks like something my mom would wear," he said. After he paid the sales clerk, Tony turned awkwardly to Andrea. "Well, thanks," he said slowly. "I guess I'll see you when school starts."

"Sure," she said, smiling. "Have a good Christmas." In a way she hated to see him leave. It had been fun shopping together. But he left in a hurry and soon was lost among the throng of shoppers.

"You know," Terri remarked, "he seemed almost human today. Why can't he be like that in school?"

Andrea shrugged. "A lot of things aren't what they seem," she said absently. Then she pushed Terri toward the escalator before her friend could ask a bunch of questions.

🐾 🐾 🐾 🐾 🐾 🐾 🐾

Andrea was nervous. It was already past four o'clock on Christmas Day, and her dad still hadn't stopped by the house. "He'll be here," her mom kept saying, but she kept eyeing the mantle clock, too.

Andrea scanned the neat stack of gifts opened and displayed under the tree. Her mom had bought her a beautiful blue sweater, khaki cords, and a purse. Timmy had given her a canvas lunch bag and hair clips. She loved her gifts, appreciating how much they must have cost.

Timmy sat on the floor, playing with his new set of building blocks. It was hard for his uncoordinated hands to stack them. But he tried over and over without getting frustrated and angry as he usually did when a task seemed too hard for him.

If only my dad would come, Andrea thought. It had been a good Christmas, but a lonely one. She kept remembering past Christmases, when her dad would read the Christmas story from the Bible and play Santa Claus, passing out the gifts, pretending he couldn't read the name tags until everyone was overwhelmed with excitement.

She recalled the time he'd sat up half the night putting together Timmy's first tricycle. She thought of him carving the turkey, falling asleep on the sofa during the afternoon football game, making turkey and cranberry sandwiches for himself and Andrea just before bedtime on Christmas night. She remembered so many things, so many good times.

She might have started crying if the doorbell hadn't rung. She flew to the door and flung it open. Her dad stood there holding their gifts. "Ho-ho-ho!" he cried merrily.

"Daddy!" Andrea shouted, flinging her arms around him. "Mom! Timmy! Dad's here!"

"Hello, Jim," her mom said tersely, drying her hands on a dish towel as she came in from the kitchen.

"Beth," he said, nodding toward her.

"You're late," Andrea's mom added. "The kids had about given up on you."

"Don't start on me," he warned.

Andrea's heart dropped. *Don't have an argument now, not on Christmas Day!*

"It's all right," Andrea said quickly. "You're here now. Let's open presents," she urged as she pulled her dad toward the Christmas tree.

Under the tree she pulled the gift she'd chosen and lovingly wrapped for her dad. "Here," she said, handing him the present.

He tore off the paper, held up the book, examined it, and announced, "Thanks, honey. It's a great choice. I like a good spy story."

He gave Andrea a pale pink sweater and denim skirt. He gave Timmy a soft football and a bright red helmet. Timmy was thrilled. He donned his helmet and ran up the stairs, clutching the ball under his arm.

"I held dinner for you," Andrea's mom began.

"You shouldn't have," Mr. Manetti told her. "I can't stay."

"But, Daddy!" Andrea cried.

"What do you mean you can't stay?" her mom asked with irritation in her voice. "We've been waiting all day. I've kept dinner on hold. You can't just drop by, open gifts, and then leave."

"I'm sorry," he said, looking at Andrea. "But I've got to catch a plane to Ontario tonight. There's a business meeting first thing in the morning. Work doesn't stop—even for the holidays."

"This stinks, Jim!" Andrea's mom said angrily.

Things weren't going as Andrea had hoped. She'd imagined a whole evening of sitting around like a regular family—spending time together and talking. Now, her dad was leaving.

"Can't you stay longer, Daddy?" she asked. "Please?"

"I can't, honey. But I'll be back next week. I'll take you to lunch. All right?"

Tears welled up in Andrea's eyes. All she could do was nod. Her mom followed her dad to the door. She could hear them arguing. "I don't appreciate this one bit, Jim," her mom said. "Christmas Day and you can't spend it with your kids."

"It's not like I have a choice!" And it continued for several more minutes.

Andrea pressed her hands to her ears. She didn't want to hear them anymore. *This is the worst Christmas I've ever had,* she told herself. *My parents will never get back together. Never!*

Then she ran up to her room and slammed the door behind her.

EIGHT

Everyone in the choral room seemed to be talking at once. Ms. Vesper had just made a startling announcement. In the spring the class would be presenting a full-scale production of the musical *Grease*.

Andrea could barely contain her excitement. Being able to do an entire show, complete with makeup, lights, and staging seemed too good to be true.

More than anything, she wanted to have a singing role in this show. Deep down, she wanted the part of Sandy, the lead. "I can do that part!" she told herself.

Andrea concentrated on what Ms. Vesper was saying. "I want all of you to try out for any part you feel you're qualified to play," she told the students. "There are lots of parts available. It's a big cast. And I think I have a lot of talent in this room.

"I will hold open auditions. There are also a lot of jobs for your friends who'd like to help out behind the scenes. We have scenery to build and paint. We need makeup people. There's plenty of work for everybody, and I'd like to get the entire school involved in the show's production, if possible.

"We'll need to put up posters, do some public service spots on local radio stations, and invite the whole community. It's my plan to use the profits from ticket sales on new music, show choir outfits, and class supplies. Besides," she paused, "I think we'll have a lot of fun doing *Grease*."

Some of the kids clapped. Others yelled, "Cool!" and "All right!" The entire idea was met with unanimous approval.

Ms. Vesper continued. "I have about thirty copies of the actual script. I want those of you who think you want to try out for the leads and the other major roles to pick up a copy after class today. Take it home, decide which part you want to try out for, and start memorizing some lines.

"I'll hold tryouts beginning next Wednesday. I want to start rehearsals in two weeks. I'd like to have *Grease* ready for an audience by mid-April. That gives us about three months to do the job. Think we can do it?"

The class immediately began to buzz with chatter as students talked about which roles they wanted and who would be cast. Ms. Vesper laughed and held up her hands for silence. "Then get out there and talk it up," she urged. "I want full participation from you. Remember," she shouted, "*Grease* is the word!"

As the class broke up, Andrea went down front to pick up a copy of the script. She watched Tony from the corner of her eye. She didn't know how to act around him. He had ignored her in the halls whenever she walked by him. He barely acknowledged her in class. Since he no longer rode the school bus, she didn't see him before or after school. Still, she wanted to ask how his mom had liked the scarf they'd chosen together over the Christmas holidays. But she was afraid to approach him.

As she passed him near the piano, he bumped up against her. "Hey!" he said loudly. "Watch where you're going!" he barked.

"I-I didn't mean to," Andrea said, confused.

"Sure you did," he said accusingly as a couple of his friends looked on. "I tell you, girls can't seem to keep their hands off me!" he announced. The group of guys laughed.

Andrea blushed. How could Tony behave so nicely one time and so mean and childish another? It didn't make sense.

"Sorry," she said coldly to Tony and the group of guys around him. While they continued to laugh and joke, Andrea picked up a copy of the script. Then she gave Tony a long, angry look and left the choral room.

Later, at home in her room, Andrea put on her *Grease* soundtrack, flipped through the thick script, and began to highlight the parts for Sandy. She knew she couldn't sing like Olivia Newton-John, but she could sing. She was wondering about her competition for the part when the phone rang downstairs.

She ran down the steps and picked up the phone. It was Terri.

"Memorized your part yet?" Terri teased. It was all they had talked about on the bus ride home.

"I'm working on it," Andrea said. "Are you going to do something for the show?"

"How about makeup?" Terri asked. "I think that would be fun. Don't you?"

"You would do a great job," Andrea said. "Look at all the secret practice you've had."

Terri giggled. "I know. Listen, I'll help you memorize your lines if you want."

"That'd be great!" Andrea cried. "Thanks a lot." She looked at the clock. "Oh, my gosh!" she exclaimed. "It's almost time for Mom and Timmy to be home. I haven't even put supper on! I have to go."

She hung up and hurried into the kitchen. She quickly got out a pan and ingredients so she could get dinner started before her mom drove up. "How am I supposed to do it all?" she asked herself grimly. "How can I do all my home chores, my homework, and be in a show all at the same time?"

She didn't know, but she had to try. The thought of the musical was the only bright spot in her life right now. She didn't even see her dad very much because he was always "busy." And she missed him a lot.

Andrea began to have the nagging feeling that her parents' breakup was somehow partly her fault. *If only I'd been a better daughter*, she thought, *then maybe they wouldn't have fought so much. If only I had tried harder to keep them from fighting, maybe we would still be together.* Her mind ran around in circles.

"I want that part of Sandy," she said aloud to the pan of frying hamburgers. The truth was she *needed* that part!

🐾 🐾 🐾 🐾 🐾 🐾 🐾

Andrea was so nervous. She sat in the choral room with about fifteen other kids, all of whom were waiting for their turns to audition for *Grease*. She'd heard that Kathy Parley was trying out for the Sandy role. Kathy was a ninth grader. She was tall and kind of pretty, but her voice wasn't very strong.

She was sure that Paula Winski would get the part of Rizzo, the tough girl leader of the Pink Ladies. She looked the part with her leather jacket, frizzy brown hair, and bright red lipstick. She sang well, too.

When it came time for Andrea to audition, her heart was pounding so hard that she was sure Ms. Vesper could hear it. But once she started reading Sandy's lines, she felt calmer.

"Very good," Ms. Vesper said when she'd read about three pages of dialogue. "Now, how about a song?"

Andrea nodded. "I've been working on 'Hopelessly Devoted to You,'" she said softly.

"I've got the music right here," Ms. Vesper said, turning the pages of the musical score on her piano. She played the opening chords, and Andrea began to sing. Her voice was strong as she concentrated on her delivery of the beautiful ballad.

When Andrea was finished, she felt good about her performance. She only hoped that it had been good enough to get the part.

"Thanks, Andrea," Ms. Vesper told her. "I'll be posting the parts next week."

"Thanks," Andrea said. Then she picked up her books and left. She wanted to stay and hear her competition, but it was getting late. She had already missed the school bus and was going to have to catch the city bus home. She'd told her mom about the tryouts, but her mom hadn't seemed very interested. Still, she told Andrea she could do it, as long as she came straight home and started supper.

At the bus stop, Andrea shivered in the cold January air. She stamped her feet. They felt frozen. *Where is the dumb bus anyway?* She'd been waiting for more than ten minutes in the gray, slushy snow.

She was so busy looking down the street that she didn't notice a guy approaching her. "Waiting on the bus?" he asked.

"Oh!" Andrea cried, nearly jumping off the ground. She turned and faced Tony Columbo. The raw wind ruffled through his dark hair and turned his cheeks rosy. His dark eyes stared bright and hard at her.

"Y-you scared me," she stammered.

"The bus won't be here for a while. Let's walk down to the pizza place and get a slice," he said. It sounded more like a command than an invitation.

Andrea felt suddenly flustered. She was alone on the street, it was starting to get dark, and Tony was urging her to go off with him. She was still a little afraid of him.

"I don't think so," she mumbled, looking down at the ground. She was hesitant to meet his sullen look.

"It's cold," he stated flatly. "Let's not stand here all night. Come on."

"Thanks," she said. "But I can't."

"Scared?" he taunted.

"No!" she snapped, looking up at him. "I-I just don't want to."

He eyed her again, shrugged, and said, "Suit yourself. But I'm not asking you again." Then he ambled off down the street.

Andrea watched him walk away and felt a pang of regret. She hadn't been very nice to him. And it would have been fun to go sit down and have a slice of pizza. But she'd blown it. She sighed, clutched her books, and shivered.

"Isn't anything ever going to go right for me?" she asked herself.

NINE

Andrea spent the entire week on pins and needles. A part of her couldn't wait for Ms. Vesper to announce the parts for *Grease*. Another part of her dreaded the announcement. She was afraid that she would not get the part of Sandy. It was the only part she wanted.

"I got a promotion today," her mother said one night during supper. Andrea stopped eating and looked at her mother's beaming face.

"That's great, Mom," she said.

"Great, Mom," Timmy echoed.

"I get my own desk at the bank," she continued. "I'll be helping customers open new accounts. I'll make more money, too. I've only been there a few months, and I already got a promotion." Andrea could tell that her mother felt very pleased with herself.

Andrea didn't know what else to say. She was glad her mom had gotten a promotion. But she couldn't help wondering what her dad was doing that night. Was he thinking about them? Did he miss them?

Andrea changed the subject. "If I get the part in the show, can I take it?" she asked.

"The show?" her mother asked.

She doesn't even remember, Andrea thought sadly. "The school musical, you know, *Grease?*"

"When are rehearsals?" her mom asked.

"After school, four days a week, and on Saturdays nine till noon," Andrea said.

"Oh, honey, that's so much time . . . ," her mom started. "What about your school work?"

"I can do it all," Andrea pleaded. "I want this part. I really want to do it. Please, Mom!"

"How would you get home every day? You'll miss the school bus."

"The city bus stops right outside the school. I can take it."

"I don't know," her mom said, shaking her head.

"Oh, please!" Andrea begged again.

"Well, you haven't gotten the part yet. So let's wait and see."

Andrea wanted her to say "yes" now, while she was in such a good mood about her promotion. She pleaded with her one more time.

"Oh, I guess we could work something out," her mom finally said.

Andrea smiled broadly. Her mom had said everything but yes! Now, all she had to do was land the role in the show.

🐾 🐾 🐾 🐾 🐾 🐾 🐾

Andrea's heart pounded as she approached the list posted on the bulletin board in the choral room. Typed at the top of the list was "Parts for *GREASE*," and right below that was "Sandy . . . Andrea Manetti."

She'd gotten the part! She felt like doing handsprings! She looked at the paper again, just to make sure. Her name was there all right, along with several others, including Paula Winski, who got the part of Rizzo. "Strange," she muttered. There was no name next to the role of Danny, the male lead. *I guess Ms. Vesper hasn't assigned that part yet.*

Other students crowded around her. Most seemed pleased for her, and she was pleased with herself. She couldn't wait to tell her family.

Suddenly, she got an idea. Instead of going straight home after school, she'd hop a city bus and go over to her dad's apartment.

She knew where it was. She'd been there once before. It was a big, nine-story, redbrick building on the south side. It was an adults-only complex, but kids could visit. They just couldn't live there. Her dad's apartment was on the seventh floor and had a view of factories and the expressway. Further in the distance, you could see the tall buildings of downtown.

"I'll surprise him," Andrea told herself excitedly. He'd said that she could come visit any time. He'd be at home, she knew, because she'd talked to him on the phone the night before.

"Hey! Good luck!" he'd said when she'd told him about trying out for the part in the musical. "I'll be pulling for you, honey." He sounded so excited for her, happier than her mother had sounded about the show.

"That's exactly what I'll do," she said to herself. "I'll catch the bus to Dad's apartment and surprise him."

Maybe, after they talked, he would take her home in his car, she hoped. And maybe he would stay for supper. And maybe, now that her mother had a promotion and a raise, they could talk and have a good time with each other again. Andrea grew more and more excited. She couldn't wait for the school bell to ring.

🐜 🐜 🐜 🐜 🐜 🐜 🐜

Andrea stood in the apartment lobby, waiting for the elevator to reach the ground floor. She was having second thoughts about going to her dad's apartment. It had taken her much longer to get there on the bus than she had planned.

Inside, the lobby needed a coat of paint. The man behind the front desk leaned on his elbows. A newspaper was propped in front of him. Three people sat in the lobby. They looked vacantly at her as she walked by them.

The elevator arrived with a groan, and Andrea quickly stepped inside. She was grateful that there was no one else on it. She pushed the button for the seventh floor and waited while the old elevator car lurched its way upward. She got off and walked hesitantly down the hallway to apartment 709. She paused outside the door. Her hands were shaking.

Why do I feel so nervous? Andrea wondered. She had every right to be there. After all, her father lived here! She knocked on the door, softly. There was no answer. She tried again, this time a little louder. There was still no answer.

She felt disappointed and was turning away when the door finally opened. A woman stood in the doorway. She was young, blonde, and dressed in a short skirt. Andrea had never seen her before.

"What do you want, honey?" the woman asked, looking Andrea over.

"Excuse me," Andrea mumbled. "I must have the wrong apartment." She looked at the door. The number was 709. "My—my dad . . . ," she stammered.

"You must be Andrea," the woman said with a toothy smile. "Jim's told me all about you. Come on in." The woman took Andrea's arm and pulled her inside the apartment.

Andrea felt panic well up inside her. She looked around. It was her dad's stuff. Then she saw the dining room table. It was set for two.

"Jim!" the woman called. "Andrea's here."

Her father emerged from down the hall. He was still fresh from taking a shower. *What's going on?* Andrea asked herself. *Who is this woman?*

"Andi!" her dad cried, approaching her. "I-I didn't expect you," he stammered. "What a surprise. I wish you would have called first. I've got company tonight." He was embarrassed. Andrea could tell. She'd certainly surprised him!

Andrea felt hot tears of anger well up inside her. *He's got company all right! A date!*

He tried to cover over the awkward moment. "I see you've already met Jill."

Andrea began backing toward the door. She felt like the walls were closing in on her. She had to get out of there! "I'm sorry," she said, fumbling behind her for the doorknob.

"Wait, Andi," her dad said. He reached out to her. But Andrea didn't want him touching her. She just wanted to get away.

"I have to go!" she cried. She flung open the door and ran down the hall to the elevator door. She repeatedly pressed the elevator call button as her father ran toward her.

"Honey, please come back. Let's talk," he pleaded.

The elevator door slid open in front of her. "No, no, not now, I'm sorry." She hurried into the elevator, leaving him standing in the hallway.

When she got to the ground floor, she ran out of the building and into the icy cold air to the bus stop. There she stopped, her lungs burning.

"How could he?" she asked over and over. "How could he?" She began to sob as the cars whooshed by through the wet, gray slush.

TEN

Andrea sat alone dabbing her eyes in the darkened living room. She was exhausted and so deep in thought that she didn't hear the front door open and her mother and Timmy come inside.

"Andi!" her mom called. "Andi! Why are the lights off? I know I paid the electric bill."

Andrea jumped up and turned on a lamp.

"Are you all right?" her mom asked. "Isn't dinner started? Did you just get home, too?"

"Sorry," Andrea called, quickly turning her back on her mom and rushing off into the kitchen. "The time just got away from me."

Andrea fumbled with the pots from the cupboards and ducked her head into the refrigerator. She was desperately trying to concentrate on getting dinner together.

Her mom came into the kitchen after turning on the TV for Timmy and stood next to her daughter. Her arms were crossed, and a puzzled look was on her face. "What's going on?" she asked.

Andrea turned her back and tried to keep busy. She tried to avoid her mom's probing stare. "I said, I forgot," she told her mother.

"Stop, Andi," her mom said, grabbing her arm lightly. "I want an explanation."

Andrea spun and faced her mother. Suddenly, new tears formed in her eyes and began to spill down her cheeks. "I went to see Dad today," she whispered, "to tell him I got the part in the show."

Her mom's back stiffened. "And?" she said, softening slightly at the sight of Andrea's tears.

"And there was another woman with him," she finished.

Her mom stood very still and said nothing. From the living room Andrea could hear the sound of Timmy's cartoon show.

"Well, it certainly didn't take him long," her mom finally said, bitterly and mostly to herself.

"Oh, Mom," Andrea cried. Suddenly, she was in her mom's arms. Her mother stiffened, then cautiously put her arms around her daughter's shaking shoulders. She held her for a few minutes, stroking her hair.

Andrea couldn't remember a time when her mother had held her like that. But it felt good and comforting. After a long time, her mom finally said, "Look, baby, I know it was hard on you. I'm sorry. But now that the divorce is final, your father is allowed to date other women."

Andrea wasn't sure if her mother was talking to her or to herself. Andi pulled back and rubbed her red, swollen eyes. Her mom led her over to the kitchen table, sat her down, and sat next to her. She continued to hold her daughter's hand.

"Doesn't it bother you at all?" Andrea asked, wiping her nose with a napkin. "You were *married* to each other."

Her mom sighed. "What difference does it make now?"

"Don't you still love Dad?" Andrea asked.

Her mom chose her words carefully. "A part of me will always love your father," she confirmed softly. "We had you and Timmy, didn't we? You two are the best parts of us."

"Well, I still love both of you," Andrea began. "I mean, if everybody still loves everybody, why aren't we living together?"

Her mom stood up and paced across the floor. "Sometimes love isn't enough, Andi," she said. "Sometimes it's more complicated than that."

Andrea shook her head. She didn't understand. "I thought marriage was supposed to last forever—that you promised Dad that you'd be happy forever."

Patiently, her mom tried again. "Andi, you've got to realize that life is not a fairy tale. Nothing guarantees lifelong happiness. Sometimes it's hard to understand why things happen the way they do, but when they do, you have to accept them and move on."

"Why did you get that job?" Andrea asked. "If only you hadn't wanted to go to work . . . ," her voice trailed.

"The job had nothing to do with our problems," her mom said. "It was just the last straw that proved your father and I couldn't work things out. Don't you think we tried?"

Andrea shrugged. "You were always yelling and fighting," she said.

"Yes. And I'm sorry we acted that way. We didn't think about how we were affecting you and Timmy."

Andrea began to realize her mother wasn't acting so angry anymore. Her mother was really *talking* to her. She wasn't blaming Andrea's father for all their problems. Andrea began to think that maybe the divorce wasn't totally her mother's fault after all.

"Now, Andi," her mom began. "Please don't let all of this affect your schoolwork and our life here."

"What do you mean?" Andrea asked.

"Are you going to ignore school and worry about your dad and me?" her mom asked, half-joking but with a serious tone to her question.

"I don't know," Andrea said puzzled.

"Do you know what I think?" her mom asked, smiling at Andrea. "I think it's time that we got back to living our lives again."

"What do you mean?" Andrea asked, seeing a look of determination on her mother's face.

"I think we've sat around dwelling on the past too long. It's time we made a truce and started being a family again—just you, Timmy, and me."

Andrea looked at her mother. She knew that her mother was right. Andrea had to stop being angry with her parents. She had to forgive them both and go on with her life.

"Honey, I'm glad about your part in the show," her mom added sincerely. "I think it'll be good for you to concentrate on something besides your dad and me. I want you to take the part. I'll help you make rehearsals. We'll do the chores together on Saturday afternoons. I just know you'll be terrific. I can't wait until opening night," she said proudly.

"Do you really mean it?" Andrea asked, momentarily forgetting her unhappiness.

"Of course, I mean it," her mom said and smiled. "We have to support each other, don't we?" she asked. "I love you, Andi. I really do."

That's what Dad told me the day he left, Andrea thought. Love—it was a strange emotion. It could put people on mountains. It could pull them into deep pits. And it could change. It could start out one way and end up another, like her mom and dad's love. She hoped their love for her wouldn't change.

She was glad she'd talked with her mom. It *had* made her feel better. She also understood something else. She realized that when people change, their lives need to change, too. She wasn't angry with her mother anymore about the divorce. She was still hurt by it. But Andrea realized her parents' problems didn't have anything to do with her after all.

🐾 🐾 🐾 🐾 🐾 🐾 🐾

Ms. Vesper began to practice the singing parts of *Grease* with the cast members. But she still hadn't cast the part of Danny Zuko, the male lead. Andrea began to wonder if she was ever going to choose a boy for the role.

A few students had tried out, but no one was quite right for the part. Either a guy looked right for the role, or he could sing. No one could seem to do both. For a while it looked as if Adam Roarke might get it. But he was so short. Andrea could stand next to him and look right over the top of his head. She couldn't imagine singing a romantic ballad down to a guy.

Terri helped Andrea memorize her speaking lines. Terri also signed up to do makeup and paint the props and scenery that some volunteers from shop class were making. In fact, everything was in place, except for one small detail—who was going to play Danny?

Andrea had just finished working with Ms. Vesper on some of her songs for the show when she came out of the choral room and found Terri waiting for her. Her best friend had a smile so big, it looked like her cheeks might burst.

"Guess what!" Terri cried when she saw Andrea.

"You're catching the city bus with me?" Andrea asked, surprised to see Terri still hanging around so long after school.

"I *had* to tell you the news," Terri said, ignoring Andrea's question. "Guess what?" she tried again.

"I give up. What?" asked Andrea, laughing.

"Tony Columbo's going to get suspended from school!" said Terri joyously.

"What?" Andrea asked in disbelief. "You're kidding." She remembered that he had not been in chorus that day. He skipped his other classes all the time, but he always made it to Ms. Vesper's class.

"It's true," Terri continued. "Tony and Josh Rosen got into a fight in the cafeteria today. It was so bad that it took two teachers to pull them off each other. Mr. Grimes said he was going to suspend them both!"

Somehow Andrea wasn't as delighted by the news as she thought she would be. It was true that Tony hassled her all the time. But he had a different side, too. She'd seen it at Christmas time. And she'd never forgotten what Ms. Vesper had told her about him. "Wow," Andrea said. "That's too bad."

"You are kidding, aren't you?" Terri asked in disbelief. "I thought you'd be thrilled—especially after the way he treated you when we got back from winter break. He's such a *pain*," Terri said, rolling her eyes.

"I know," Andrea agreed. "But, suspended . . ."

They rode the bus home, and Andrea stopped off at Terri's before going on to her house.

"Andrea!" Mrs. Chambers cried. "How nice you look."

"Thanks," Andrea said and smiled. She had always liked Terri's mom. She couldn't help remembering all the times she'd wished her own mother was more like her. "So, Terri tells me you're a star," Mrs. Chambers said, beaming.

Andrea blushed. "Not really." she said. "I just got a part in the school musical."

"Well, you can bet the Chambers family will be there on opening night! You always sing so well. I just know you'll be wonderful."

Later, as Andrea arrived home, she saw her mom's car in the driveway. Inside, Timmy sat watching TV. Her mom was in the kitchen fixing dinner. Andrea almost didn't recognize her.

"Your hair!" she gasped.

"Do you like it?" her mom asked, almost shyly.

Andrea stared. Her mom's once mousy-colored hair was now a rich shade of auburn. It was shortened in a style just like one of the actresses in her magazines. "It looks great!" Andrea exclaimed. She really meant it, too. It made her mom look years younger.

"Timmy almost wouldn't come to me when I picked him up at school today," her mom said with a chuckle. "I've been thinking about doing it for a while now, so I took half a day off and had it done. I used the gift certificate I got at Christmas to buy myself some new clothes, too. I'll show them to you after supper."

Andrea noticed that her mother's makeup looked fresh—brighter and more modern.

"Complete makeover," she confessed. "What do you think of the new me?"

"I like it—lots," Andrea said honestly. Her mom had never looked better. Andrea wished her dad could see her mom now. She certainly looked prettier than that woman, Jill. In fact, she looked pretty enough that he might fall in love with her all over again.

❧ ❧ ❧ ❧ ❧ ❧ ❧

The main cast clustered around the piano in the choral room, waiting for Ms. Vesper to arrive. She'd told them all that she had an important announcement about the show.

"Hope it's good news," Paula said.

"Yeah, like when we're going to start rehearsals on the stage in the gym," Mike Hudson said. He was playing the part of Kenickie, Danny's best friend.

The speculation ended when Ms. Vesper breezed into the room. "Sorry I'm late," she apologized. "Thanks for waiting. But I think I have some very good news for all of you." She paused. "I've *finally* found someone to play the part of Danny."

Everyone began to ask, "Who?"

"Come on in, *Danny*," she called to the closed door.

Everyone waited.

"I said, 'Come on . . .'"

The door swung open with a thud, and in walked Tony Columbo.

ELEVEN

*T*ony scowled at everyone as he sauntered into the room and plopped down in a chair. He stretched out, draping his arms over the backs of the chairs on either side of him. He glared defiantly at the surprised faces staring at him.

Andrea felt her own heart doing dull thuds against her chest. *It couldn't be true! Ms. Vesper couldn't mean it! How could she have picked Tony Columbo to play the part?* It was obvious by his attitude that he didn't want to do the role.

"You may as well know," Ms. Vesper said, "that Tony was my choice for the part of Danny from the very beginning."

The rest of the cast exchanged glances. Tony leaned further back in his chair and continued to look hostile. Ms. Vesper continued, "But when I asked him about assuming the role, Tony told me that he was 'too busy.'"

"I still am," Tony said curtly.

Ms. Vesper shot him a warning glance. "Yes," she said. "It seems that he was busy getting into fights." She turned her attention back toward the small cluster of cast members.

"I have asked Mr. Grimes to allow Tony to be in the show. I told him that I would be responsible for his behavior."

"Yo, Tony. Some kids get detention—and some get sentenced to musicals, eh?" someone called out.

Tony shifted in his chair and sighed. Paula gave Andrea an inquiring look. Andrea shrugged. Her palms felt clammy, and her mouth was dry. She would be the one most affected by Ms. Vesper's decision.

"Now," Ms. Vesper began, "Tony has some catching up to do. Most of you know your lines and your songs. Next week, I want to start blocking on the gym stage. Tony will be working with me on his music and lines every morning before school starts." He groaned his displeasure, and she ignored him. "Then we'll all work together after school to start putting this show together. We have just over two months' time to do this. Any questions?"

About a million, Andrea thought. Working with Tony Columbo wasn't going to be easy—not only because of his attitude now, but also because of their history. But there was nothing she could do about it. The decision had been made. Andrea sighed, picked up her books, and headed for the door. It was going to be a *long* time until opening night!

🐚 🐚 🐚 🐚 🐚 🐚 🐚

Blocking for the show was a slow and tedious process. It took hours for Ms. Vesper to set up each scene and mark the floor with chalk so the actors would remember where to stand when delivering their lines.

They worked on the small scenes first. "We'll bring in the ensemble toward the end of rehearsals," Ms. Vesper told them. The ensemble was going to fill in as the other students of the fictional Rydell High School. They would sing and dance around the central cast.

While Tony was hardly pleasant to them, he at least was cooperative. Andrea began to wonder if he was secretly enjoying himself. He still went out of his way to be disruptive and provoke

Andrea. Whenever they stood next to each other he always seemed to "accidentally" step on her foot. Or he would shove up against her and cause her to lose her balance.

Yet, the first time they performed a song together, the effect was magic. Tony's voice complimented Andrea's beautifully. They blended in perfect harmony when they sang. Ms. Vesper was very pleased. So were the rest of the cast members.

After a particularly energetic rendition of "Summer Love," everybody clapped. Andrea blushed. Tony bowed arrogantly from his waist.

One afternoon, just as rehearsal was ending, Andrea heard someone call her name from one of the gym bleachers. She was surprised, mostly because Ms. Vesper always insisted on closed rehearsals. No one was allowed to watch the actors work. The cast felt less self-conscious rehearsing without an audience, plus it heightened interest in the show for the rest of the school.

"Andi!" the man's voice called again. She looked down from the stage to see her father approaching. She caught her breath. *What is he doing here?* she wondered.

He smiled up at her and said, "You look terrific up there! And you sound even better!"

She smiled weakly. She was glad to see him, but she was still upset about discovering his girlfriend. "Hi, Dad." she mumbled.

"Give you a lift home?" he asked.

"I usually take the bus," she said, coming down off the stage, gathering her books, and walking toward the double gym doors.

"My car's right outside," he persisted.

From the corner of her eye, Andrea could see Tony watching her. She hadn't told anyone at school about her parents' divorce—not even Terri. And she didn't want anyone to know now, especially Tony.

"Well, all right," she said quickly, as her dad fell into step next to her. "Let's go. Mom will have supper waiting." She hoped they sounded like a normal father and daughter heading home for dinner.

When they were outside, her dad said, "I've missed you, Andi."

She felt her resentment over their last meeting rise again.

"I tried to call you the night you left my apartment," he said. "But your mom thought it best to give you some time to adjust and come to grips with the situation."

Andrea felt both touched and angry over her mother's protectiveness. "It's okay," she told him. "I understand. You're divorced now. You can date if you want."

"Honey," he said, opening the car door for her. "You're very important to me. I care what you think and how you feel."

She couldn't think of anything to say, so she slid across the cold seat and waited for him to get in and start the car. They rode a while in silence.

"Have you seen Mom lately?" Andrea asked.

"Uh, no," he said. "But I talk to her on the phone every week about you and Timmy."

"She's changed," Andrea said. "She's fixed herself up. She looks real pretty now."

"When I first met her, she was very pretty," he mused. "I'm glad she's fixing herself up again."

Andrea's interest perked up. An idea began to take shape in her mind. "Do you have time to come in?" she asked as his car pulled into the driveway.

"No, not tonight," he said. "I just wanted to see you today. I wanted to explain about Jill and me. I didn't want you to be mad and upset."

She tried to be angry with him, but she couldn't. All she felt was confusion. She loved both of her parents, and she wanted them to love each other again more than anything. Andrea sighed and leaned over to kiss her father. "Thanks," she said. "I've missed you. I'm not mad any more."

"Good!" he smiled and kissed her forehead. "I'll make plans to pick you up soon. We'll go to a movie, just you and me."

"I'd like that," she said.

"You're going to be great in that show! Don't forget to tell me when it opens. I don't want to miss my little star's big night!" Andrea's dad called as she closed the car door behind her.

"I won't," Andrea promised. Then she hurried up the steps of the porch. She remembered the article she read months ago about the celebrity couple that had reunited, and the hope she had felt then rekindled. She had a plan. . . .

TWELVE

*A*ndrea was tired. Her voice was tired. Her eyes were tired. Her whole body was tired. In fact, everybody on the set was tired—and irritable.

Ms. Vesper had a terrible cold. She kept trying to give directions between coughs and sneezes. The rehearsal wasn't going very well. With the performance less than six weeks away, it seemed they would never be ready.

The props still weren't finished. Terri had helped paint those that had been built the previous Saturday. But the shop class volunteers were still working on the rest of them. Andrea began to wonder if *Grease* was ever going to have an opening night.

"All right," Ms. Vesper said through a tissue. "Let's try the drive-in scene." Andrea had been dreading this scene. This was the part where Danny was supposed to try to kiss Sandy. As Tony and she took their places on the side-by-side metal chairs on the stage, she could feel her heart pounding. Her palms felt clammy.

It wasn't that she was afraid of Tony. In fact, it was more that she was becoming attracted to him. Working with him every day, like she had been, was proving to her that he was a much different person from the tough guy image he tried to project.

Tony still tried to annoy her a lot. But when he let his guard down, he was different. He was a sensitive guy. Being near him sometimes made Andrea's heart jump or caused her stomach to flip-flop.

"Now remember," Ms. Vesper said after she finished coughing. "This is your first real date, Sandy and Danny. You're as different as two people can be. But you're also strongly attracted to each other."

Andrea sat stiffly in her chair with her palms flat on the top of her legs. She stared straight ahead and pretended she was in the front seat of Danny's car facing a drive-in movie screen. Danny sat still, also. Then ever so slowly, he inched his arm up, cracked his knuckles, and stretched.

"Good. Good," Ms. Vesper encouraged. "Not too fast to put the moves on her. Nice and slow, Danny."

Slowly, Danny inched his arm around the shoulders of his date. Sandy watched him nervously from the corner of her eye, then clasped her hands in her lap.

"Excellent!" Ms. Vesper whispered.

Next Danny's hand began to stroke the back of Sandy's hair and rub the base of her neck. Andrea felt a tingling sensation shoot up her spine. She began to blush and to lose the character of Sandy.

"Don't fidget, Sandy," Ms. Vesper said crossly. Andrea tried to regain her concentration on her character. Sandy nervously tossed her hair and shot Danny a warning glance. She hoped he got the message from Andrea, too.

Danny let a half-smile trail over his mouth. Then he reached his other arm across in front of Sandy and locked his hands. "What are you doing?" she asked both as Sandy and Andrea.

"Checkin' the time," he said. "Movie should start soon." Then without warning, he leaned over, brought her chin up sharply, and kissed her.

Andrea shoved him hard in his chest, trying to break his hold on her.

"Tony!" Andrea could hear Ms. Vesper shout. "Stop that! I told you to just *try* to kiss her! You know that!"

The rest of the cast laughed and clapped. "Nice going," Mike Hudson yelled. "Me next?"

Andrea squirmed within Tony's strong embrace. Finally, he released her. She leaped to her feet. Her face was flushed. As she stood up, her chair hit the floor with a loud bang. "How dare you!" she yelled at him.

Tony grinned up at her and shrugged, "Just trying to set the mood, *Sandy*," he said.

"Ms. Vesper!" Andrea shouted.

But the teacher was already shouting at Tony. "That was totally uncalled for!"

"So what are you going to do?" he asked with a smirk. "Throw me out?"

"No way, Tony!" Ms. Vesper said coldly. "Are you all right, Andrea?" she asked.

Andrea was embarrassed, but she was all right. She glared at Tony and wished she had the courage to slap him.

Ms. Vesper sighed and told the cast, "Let's call it quits for today." Andrea felt relieved. She didn't think she could have tried the scene again. "I feel lousy, anyway," Ms. Vesper said. "We've got a lot of work ahead. But we'll start fresh again tomorrow. Besides, it'll do everyone good to get out of here early today."

Everybody began to talk and gather his or her things. Ms. Vesper walked up to Tony and pointed her finger at his face. Andrea noticed that, like herself, Ms. Vesper only came up to Tony's chest when she stood in front of him.

"I don't want anymore improvisations like that again, young man," she announced. "You play your part correctly. Do you understand?"

Tony shrugged and slipped on his leather jacket. "Got it," he said, grinning. Then he turned and walked out of the gym.

"You okay?" Ms. Vesper asked Andrea one more time.

"I'm all right," she said. "Maybe if I hurry, I can catch the early bus and beat my mom home. I'll see you tomorrow."

Ms. Vesper nodded. Andrea left the fantasy world of *Grease* and went outside into the blustery late March afternoon.

She arrived at the bus stop just in time to see her bus disappearing down the street. "Just what

I need!" Andrea cried. Now it would be twenty minutes before another bus would come along. She leaned against the bus stop signpost and mulled over her churning thoughts.

She could still feel Tony's lips on hers. It had made her mad. But it had also been exciting. It was the first time a boy had kissed her—really kissed her. It wasn't just a stolen peck on the cheek like David Bates had done in the sixth grade. Besides, that kiss had been on a dare anyway.

What a way to get a first kiss, she thought. She couldn't wait to tell Terri. It would probably be all over school tomorrow anyway. *Leave it to Tony Columbo to always be in the conversation.*

"You mad?"

Andrea had been so deep in thought, she hadn't heard Tony walk up next to her.

"Huh?" she cried and whirled around.

"I always seem to be scaring you," he teased. "I just want to know if you're mad about the rehearsal."

"That was pretty sneaky!" she snapped, trying to sound angrier than she felt.

"Yeah," he said. "But it was fun, wasn't it?" His dark eyes danced mischievously. "No hard feelings?" he asked and held out his hand.

"Oh, stop it," she said, giving him a half-smile.

"That's better," he told her ducking down and forcing her to look at him. "You, uh, you want to go for that slice of pizza?" he asked hesitantly.

She felt her heart beat a little faster. She really did want to go have a slice of pizza with him. "Sure!" she said suddenly.

"All right!" He gave her the benefit of his dazzling smile. "Come on."

She fell into step beside him, glancing over at him every so often. He was a puzzle! He was tough on the outside, so angry and hot-tempered. But sometimes he could be so charming, so much fun.

They arrived at the pizza place a few blocks from the school. He held the heavy glass door for her, and they went inside. She sat in a booth while he went up to the counter, ordered two pieces of pizza and two sodas, and brought them back to the table.

He sat opposite her, opened his straw, and blew the paper in her direction.

"Cut it out," she said.

"You like the show?" he asked, ignoring her remark.

"I love it," she told him.

"I do, too," he confessed, taking a long sip from his straw.

"I thought you hated the whole thing!" she said, surprised at his confession.

He shrugged. "It grows on you."

They talked for an hour, about the show, school, and their friends. Andrea forgot about catching the bus. She could have talked for hours. But it was getting late. Already, the sky outside was beginning to darken, and streetlights were flickering on.

"I have to catch the bus," she reminded Tony as she slowly gathered her books.

"I'll ride with you," he said, standing up with her. He brushed her hair off the side of her face with his hand. She felt her stomach do little flip-flops again.

"But you get off before me," she said as they went out the door and started back toward the bus stop.

"I'll ride to your stop and then walk back," he said.

"You don't have to—" she began.

"It's okay," he interrupted. "I know where you live. It isn't that far from my place."

During the bus ride home Andrea wondered how he knew—and why.

THIRTEEN

*A*ndrea stared at the calendar hanging on the kitchen wall. The idea, which had begun to form weeks before, resurfaced in her mind. This Saturday, March 8, would have been her parents' sixteenth wedding anniversary.

She wondered if either one of them would think of it—if either of them would even remember. But she did. And she thought, *What would it be like to get the two of them together?* They both had changed a lot over the past months since the divorce.

Her mom was more self-confident and less uptight, plus she looked great. Andrea's dad was doing well in business, making lots of sales for his company. Maybe, if she could get them together for one evening with no distractions, no conflicts, just maybe they would rediscover one another. Maybe they'd fall in love and get married again.

The more Andrea thought about it, the more excited she became. They had loved each other once. Surely they could fall in love again. Then they could all live together again as a family. Maybe the divorce had been a big mistake that she could help correct. It was certainly worth a try!

Andrea decided that she would fix dinner for them as a surprise. *I'll get Timmy to help*, she thought with growing excitement. Timmy could do little things. And she'd make it a game for him. They'd eat early and then set up a romantic candlelight dinner for their parents. Then, while their parents ate and gazed at each other through the glowing candles, she and Timmy would disappear upstairs and let nature take its course.

The dinner would take a lot of planning. She couldn't let either of them get any ideas of what she was up to. Andrea knew that it would work. Once her parents could just relax, they'd realize that they had loved each other all along. She was sure of it!

That evening, after supper, she casually asked, "Mom, would you mind if I brought someone special home for dinner tomorrow night? I'll cook."

"What?" her mom asked. She stopped loading the dishwasher and turned to look at Andrea. "Is there somebody in your life I don't know about?" she teased.

Andrea blushed. "In a way," she said. She was afraid to look her mom in the eye. She was afraid her mom would pry the truth out of her. "I'd just like to invite a special friend over. That's all."

"Well," her mom began. She paused, then said, "Sure! Why not? What can I do to help?"

Andrea tried to conceal her excitement. "Oh, nothing. I want to do this all by myself. I'd like it if you wouldn't even come downstairs until I get everything ready. I want it to be a surprise for you, too. Oh, and Mom," she paused, choosing her words carefully, "Could you dress up? Please?"

Mrs. Manetti stared at her daughter. "My, this friend must really be special. Who is he? I have to assume it's a 'he,'" she asked tenderly.

Andrea took a deep breath. "You'll see," she said. "It's important to me, okay?"

"Sure," her mom said. "I'll help any way I can. And if staying out of the way and dressing up is all you want me to do, then that's what I'll do."

Andrea smiled warmly and thought, *Phase one successful!*

Later she called her dad. She held her breath while the phone rang, hoping that he was at home and that Jill wouldn't answer. She got both of her wishes.

After chatting for a few minutes she said, "I'm fixing dinner tomorrow night for a friend and me. I sure would like it if you could come."

"Uh, I don't know," he said.

"Mom will be out," Andrea said quickly. She hated to lie, but she didn't want him to have any excuse for not coming.

He didn't answer right away.

"Please, Dad," she begged. "You always take me out to dinner. Can't I take you out for once?"

He laughed and said, "I guess I could come by. I'd like to meet your friend and eat a home-cooked meal. What time?"

"Seven o'clock," she said. She was thrilled. *Phase two was successful.* Now she could move on to phase three.

First, she planned the menu. She didn't want it to be too fancy. She decided on baked chicken, steamed broccoli, and baked potatoes with sour cream and butter. For dessert, she chose baked apples with vanilla ice cream. Since she would prepare most of the meal in the oven, she'd have plenty of time to work with Timmy on setting the table.

"Would you like to help tomorrow night, Timmy?" she asked. He sat in the center of his floor, clutching his raggedy teddy bear and rocking. He didn't respond. So she patiently explained it to him again. "We'll eat first," she said. "I'll fix your favorite—macaroni and cheese."

She didn't want him to start wailing when he saw her put the food on the table for their parents. Every time Timmy saw food, he thought it was for him. "I'll even make chocolate chip cookies. We'll come up here and eat them while Mom and Dad eat," she urged.

Slowly, he turned and looked into her face. She still wasn't sure if he understood. "Timmy do," he said softly. Then he returned to his private little world and began to sway and rock to his own silent rhythm. Andrea left him, closing his bedroom door behind her.

"Can I come down?" her mom called from upstairs.

"Not yet!" Andrea yelled back. "But soon! I'll let you know when we're ready."

Andrea surveyed Timmy's and her handiwork with satisfaction. They'd set the table with the best linen. She'd even put out the linen napkins. The silverware and plates glimmered in the flickering light of the two thin taper candles. Andrea had helped Timmy put a bouquet of fresh tulips into a vase and place them on the table. She had remembered her mom had once told her that she and her dad had tulips at their wedding, so Andrea had stopped by the floral shop that morning after rehearsal to buy some.

She smelled the delicious scent of dinner telling her the food was almost done. Andrea was proud of herself and Timmy because they'd done it all. Everything looked beautiful.

Timmy giggled and jumped up and down. "Surprise! Surprise!" he cried.

"Sh-sh!" she commanded. "We can't let Mom know."

Just then, the doorbell rang. They both ran to the door, and Andrea opened it. It was their dad.

"Well, hi!" he smiled, hugging them both. "Sure smells good in here."

He went into the kitchen and whistled. "Some spread! You two do all this?"

Andrea nodded. "Wait," she told her dad. "My friend is upstairs."

She ran up and knocked on her mom's door. "He's here," Andrea said, hardly containing her excitement.

"Andi," her mother said as she descended the stairs. "You look like the cat that swallowed the canary. Just who is this person?"

Mr. and Mrs. Manetti saw each other at exactly the same moment. Both of their jaws dropped. A long, awkward silence followed. Andrea's heart began to pound. Something was wrong! They didn't seem glad to see each other at all.

"Andi," her mom asked, "what's the meaning of this?"

"I fixed dinner for both of you. It-it was supposed to be a s-s-surprise . . . ," Andrea stammered.

Her dad cleared his throat. He shifted uncomfortably. "Honey," he said, "you shouldn't have. I don't know what to say."

"Andi," her mom said. "You tricked me. You made me think that someone very special was coming."

"But Dad *is* special," she cried. "Today would have been your sixteenth anniversary!"

Andrea's parents looked helplessly at each other. "I think I'd better go," her dad said, picking up his coat.

"I think so, too," her mom agreed.

"But you can't go!" Andrea cried. "I want you to have dinner together! I planned it all."

"You shouldn't have," her mom said.

Suddenly, Timmy started shouting. "Come on, Andi! Upstairs! Play with Timmy. Eat cookies."

"Stop it, Timmy!" Mrs. Manetti said curtly to her son.

"Take it easy, Beth," Andrea's dad said.

"Don't tell me how to act!" she said.

"I'd better leave," Mr. Manetti said, his face growing red.

"You can't!" Andrea wailed.

"Cookies!" Timmy kept shouting. He tugged on Andrea's arm.

Andrea felt dizzy as she watched the disaster unfold. *How could everything have gone so wrong?* Her head started to pound.

She whirled around to Timmy. "Be quiet!" she yelled. She seized him by his arm and began dragging him up to his room.

Timmy wailed louder. He kicked and tried to bite her. When they got upstairs, she put him into his room. "Stay in there!" she cried at the top of her voice.

Then she ran down the hall to her room and threw herself onto the bed. She began to sob uncontrollably.

FOURTEEN

*A*ndrea lay in her darkened room for a long time. She was exhausted. Even though she had given it all her effort, her plan to reunite her parents had failed.

Finally, she heard the door open. She felt someone sit down on her bed. Andrea rolled over and saw her mother.

"You all right?" her mom asked softly, as she began stroking Andrea's hair. "I cleaned up downstairs and put the food away. You did a terrific job with dinner."

Andrea didn't feel like saying anything. Her mom continued, "Why did you do it, Andi?"

After a moment of silence Andrea said, "I thought if you and Dad spent some time alone, it would make you guys want to live together again."

"Andi," her mother said with sigh, "you have to accept that your dad and I are divorced now. We still love and share you and Timmy, but we can't be married to each other."

Andrea said nothing.

"People aren't puppets, Andi," her mom said flatly. "You can't make them behave any way that suits you. Your dad and I made the decision to divorce. Please accept it for your own sake."

"When I get married, I'm never going to get divorced!" Andrea said fiercely.

"I hope you don't," her mom said. "It's a very hard thing to do."

Andrea sighed deeply. She sat up on her bed and asked, "Where's Dad?"

"He went home. He's very concerned about you, honey. He feels very bad about tonight. He said to tell you that he'll call you tomorrow. Neither of us were ready for your surprise. Do you understand?"

"Sure," Andrea said curtly. "It was a dumb idea."

"Why don't we go downstairs and eat the baked apples?" her mom suggested. "They looked yummy. And to be honest, I'm starved."

"Fine," Andrea said.

They went down to the kitchen. Andrea's mom dished up the apples after warming them in the microwave. She put a scoop of ice cream on each one. They ate for a few minutes in silence.

"So, tell me," her mom asked cheerfully. "How's the musical coming?"

Andrea hadn't thought about the show all evening. "Rehearsal went well this morning. We're working with all the props now," she said. "Ms. Vesper says we'll have two dress rehearsals next week. Then, it's opening night."

"I'm looking forward to seeing you in it. Your dad's coming, too. We're both very proud of you, Andi."

Andrea smiled weakly, but her mind drifted to the way she had treated Timmy earlier. *I was so mean*, she thought. It was impossible for him to understand what had been going on. "Mom, I need to tell Timmy I'm sorry," Andrea said.

"Yes, I think that's a good idea," her mom agreed. "He adores you. I'm sure he's asleep by now. But go up and check on him anyway."

Andrea pushed away from the table and went upstairs to Timmy's room. When she reached his door, her heart froze. Timmy's door was partially open! It was supposed to be closed. Even though he could walk around the house freely when other people were with him, Timmy seemed to understand that when his door was shut, he wasn't supposed to open it and wander out.

Andrea flung open the door and hurried inside. The room was empty! His bed was still made. And his overstuffed teddy bear was missing.

Andrea got chills all over. "Timmy!" she cried, running around his room. She looked under his bed. She looked inside his closet. But Timmy was gone! She had forgotten to shut his door, and he had just walked away.

"Mom!" she yelled. "Mom! Quick! I can't find Timmy! He's gone!"

Mrs. Manetti ran up the stairs. She also searched the room, calling for her son.

"Oh, Mom!" Andrea cried, wringing her hands. "I forgot to shut his door. He's gone, and it's all my fault."

Her mom started to say something, but the look of anguish on Andrea's face stopped her. "All right," she said instead. "Let's not panic. Let's search the house from top to bottom. Maybe he crawled off and fell asleep somewhere."

The two of them began a systematic search of the two-story house. Andrea looked in all of his favorite hiding places and even in places he was scared to go, like the basement. Timmy was nowhere to be found.

Her mom met her in the hallway. Her search had been unsuccessful, too. "He's not inside," she said. Andrea began to cry as she realized Timmy might have wandered away from the house altogether.

"Andi, stop," her mom said sternly. "Get the flashlight, and let's look around outside. Maybe he's around the yard."

Andrea shivered in the cold night air as she and her mom scoured the front and back yards for the missing child. They looked behind shrubs, in the play fort, and even up into trees. But they didn't find Timmy.

"What are we going to do?" Andrea asked through chattering teeth.

"Call the police," her mom said grimly. "He doesn't even have a jacket. Oh, Timmy! Where are you, baby?" she cried.

🐾 🐾 🐾 🐾 🐾 🐾 🐾

Three squad cars with flashing red and blue lights sat in front of Andrea's house. After Andrea's mom had given a description of Timmy to the police, several officers with flashlights combed the Manettis' yard and their neighbors' yards. Almost every porch light on the block was on. The police had let everyone nearby know that Timmy Manetti was missing.

Andrea sat stunned and frightened on the sofa. *Poor Timmy. He could have taken off anywhere. He could be blocks away by now. It's dark and cold. He probably feels so scared and alone. Timmy isn't like a normal kid who might try to ask someone to help him. Timmy will hide because he is scared. That's going to make him even harder to find.*

Mrs. Manetti sat down next to Andrea, grabbed her hand, and said, "I've called your father. He should be here soon."

Andrea only nodded. A detective came over to them and jotted down some notes as he asked a few more questions. "We'll find him, Mrs. Manetti," the detective reassured her. "I've got men looking for him, and your neighbors have joined in and are looking, too."

Andrea's mother smiled weakly. Andrea felt her mom's hand shaking in hers. Just then the doorbell rang, and her mom got up and answered it. A small group of people whom

Andrea didn't recognize came inside along with one of the police officers.

"Mrs. Manetti, these folks are from the media. They'd like to interview you," the officer said.

Mrs. Manetti hesitated. "It might help," one reporter said. "Maybe someone will remember seeing him and call the police."

Mrs. Manetti nodded her consent. "Okay," she said softly.

Andrea watched as cameras, men and women with microphones and notepads, and photographers flowed into the living room. Once the cameramen set up their equipment and began shooting, the reporters began to ask questions, and the photographers snapped photos. The whole time Andrea was anxious.

She heard one newswoman say into her recorder. "Little Timmy Manetti, the six-year-old mentally retarded son of recently divorced parents, Beth and Jim Manetti, is missing."

Andrea was horrified. The whole story would be on the news! Everyone in town would know! Everyone at school and in the show would know. Everyone would know all her family's business—

the divorce, her mentally retarded brother—all of the secrets she'd worked so hard to hide.

Andrea looked up as the detective came back inside the room. "We found this over on Main Street, about ten blocks south," he said softly. He was holding Timmy's teddy bear.

FIFTEEN ·

*A*ndrea hugged her missing brother's teddy bear. One of the photographers snapped a picture, but she didn't care. *Why would Timmy lose his bear?* she wondered. *What could have made him drop it? He loved his teddy. He'd had it since he was born.*

A few minutes later, her dad arrived. He frantically looked around the living room and made his way to one of the officers, who then directed him to the detective. After the detective briefed him, Andrea's dad sat next to her on the sofa. She threw her arms around his neck.

"Oh, Daddy," she cried. "I'm so sorry!"

"Shh," he said soothingly. He looked up at Andrea's mother and said, "May I speak to you in the kitchen—privately?"

Mrs. Manetti followed him into the kitchen. In a few moments, Andrea could hear the low rumble of their angry voices. *Do they have to argue now?* Andrea thought angrily.

Andrea went quickly into the kitchen and watched in dismay.

"For crying out loud!" her dad said. "Can't you even keep an eye on your own kid?"

Her mom fired back. "It was an accident! With all the fuss about dinner and all, Andi just forgot to shut his door."

"Oh, that's great!" he said sarcastically. "Blame it all on a thirteen-year-old!"

"No one's to blame!" she snapped. "It just happened."

"If you'd take care of your responsibilities here at home instead of working—" he said.

"I can't believe this! Now my job's to blame?" she shouted. "Today wasn't even a workday, Jim. It's Saturday!"

Andrea had heard enough. She cried, "Stop it! Stop it! Timmy's somewhere cold and alone in the dark, and the first thing you two do is argue! It's not right!" She was shaking with anger.

Her parents exchanged glances. She was right, and they knew it. "Sorry," her mom said curtly. Then she left the kitchen and headed for the front door.

At eleven o'clock, the news on Channel 4 had the story about Timmy. It showed the police searching the neighborhood and the Manetti family sitting around waiting. Yet, somehow to Andrea, it didn't seem to them like it was happening at all. Except that Timmy's bed was empty.

After the news, Andrea dozed off on the sofa. When her dad tried to move her up to her bed, she woke with a start. "Let me stay here," she mumbled sleepily.

Mr. Manetti agreed, and the rest of the night passed with no more news from the police. Andrea's dad brought in the morning newspaper when it hit the front walkway at six o'clock. On the bottom of the front page were Timmy's picture and a headline: "Have you seen this boy?" Next to it was a story about the recently divorced Manettis and their missing son.

The first red streaks of dawn were breaking across the sky when Andrea heard a big commotion outside the front door. She and her parents hurried out to the porch. Up the front walk came a policeman carrying a drowsy Timmy.

Andrea's mom took him gently in her arms. Mr. Manetti and Andrea crowded around and hugged him. "Oh, baby," her mom cried, tears streaming down her face. "Are you all right?"

Timmy rubbed his eyes. "Mama?" he asked. "Daddy? Andi?" He looked from face to face. "Timmy eat," he said.

Behind the officer, a man approached. The detective was with him. "Mr. and Mrs. Manetti," the detective began, "This is Mr. Phil Roberts. He lives on Broad Street. It seems that Mr. Roberts went out to get in his truck this morning and found Timmy curled up asleep on his front seat."

"I'm sorry, folks," the heavy-set trucker said. "I guess the little guy got inside late last night and fell asleep. I didn't know till I tried to leave this morning."

"It's okay. It's okay," Andrea's dad told him as he shook his hand profusely. "We're just grateful that you left your truck unlocked and he got inside it. Thanks for bringing him home."

Andrea was so glad to see Timmy that she began to weep again. "Andi cry," Timmy said.

She ruffled his hair and whispered, "Welcome home, Timmy. I'm so glad you're home!"

🐾 🐾 🐾 🐾 🐾 🐾 🐾

When Andrea awoke, it was after lunchtime on Monday. After the exhausting events of the weekend, Mrs. Manetti had let Andrea sleep late. She barely remembered hearing the phone ringing off and on while she slept. Her mom told her many friends and even strangers had called after seeing the news and reading yesterday's paper. While she was eating a snack and getting ready to go back to school for the remainder of her classes, her mom stuck her head into the kitchen and said, "Andi, Terri's on the phone."

Andrea went into the hallway and picked up the phone. "Hi," she said softly, thinking about what her best friend might say to her.

"You all right?" Terri asked. "I wanted to come by the second I heard about Timmy, but my mom said 'no.' She said your house was probably crawling with people, and you didn't need any more." She paused, then continued, "I called a few times this morning, but your mom said you were sleeping. You sure you're okay?"

"I'm fine," Andrea said. She felt tense.

Now that Terri had probably read the newspaper or saw the news, including the part about her parents' divorce, Andrea wasn't sure what to say to her best friend. She had never told Terri about the divorce. Even though Andrea wanted to, she never could bring herself to say it aloud.

"I know I should have told you about my parents," Andrea blurted suddenly. "But, but . . ." A lump rose into her throat.

"It's okay," Terri assured her. "Really, it's all right. I understand."

Relief washed over Andrea. "Do you?" she asked.

"Sure. My mom and I talked. She explained to me how hard it would have been for you to tell anyone. She also said to tell you that she cares a lot about you and that you've been like a daughter to her."

In a way Andrea was glad that Terri's family knew. Andrea had always loved and admired them. She'd hated keeping such a big secret from them.

"You coming to school today?" Terri asked.

"Yeah," Andrea said. "I've got to go to rehearsal after school, so Mom's going to drop me off for sixth period chorus. I'll call you tonight after I get home from rehearsal. Okay?"

"Sure," Terri told her. "Good luck." She hung up.

Actually, Andrea was dreading going to school. Now everyone would know about her personal life. Even though Terri had been so understanding, Andrea was sure others would not be. She hated that thought. But she had to go to rehearsal.

Her mom dropped her off at school. Andrea took a deep breath and went inside the choral room. She felt all eyes turning toward her as she made her way to her seat. She could also hear kids whispering and knew they were all talking about her.

"Hey, Manetti," Brian called as she passed by him. "Saw you in the newspaper. I didn't know you had a retard for a brother."

She felt her cheeks grow hot. She wanted to slug Brian in his big mouth. Suddenly, Tony's voice cut through the air.

"So what's it to you?" Tony asked. There was a challenge in both his voice and his eyes.

Brian looked at Tony for a moment, sensing Tony's warning to him to back off. He shrugged. "Nothing," Brian said. "Nothing at all, Tony."

Nobody else said a word. Andrea smiled gratefully at Tony. Then she hurried to her seat just as the bell rang, and Ms. Vesper swept into the room.

SIXTEEN

The final dress rehearsal for *Grease* was a total disaster. Kids forgot their cues. The dance scene ran long. The backdrop for the big car race fell over. And Paula, "Rizzo" in the show, went hoarse.

Yet Ms. Vesper appeared calm. Andrea, on the other hand, wanted to cry. With the show only one night away, everything was going wrong. "Don't worry," Ms. Vesper called out after the terrible dress rehearsal. "The worse things go for the final rehearsal, the better things will go on opening night!"

"In that case, we'll be ready for Broadway," Tony chirped sarcastically. Everyone laughed nervously. Andrea went home tired and worn-out, but very excited, too. Tomorrow was opening night!

The show promised to be one of the biggest things to come to the town in months. The scene the cast had performed for the Friday school assembly had been a hit, and many students had bought tickets afterward. Public service spots on the local stations had proven successful, too, as the remaining tickets had already sold out.

"You will be there?" Andrea anxiously asked her father over the telephone Saturday morning.

"Wouldn't miss it for the world!" he said. "I was thinking of coming a little early and giving the big star a good-luck kiss. How would that be?"

"Oh, Daddy," Andrea told him. "Stop teasing me. I'm not a big star."

"You are to me," he said.

"Well, the cast has to be there by five-thirty to get into makeup and costumes. I could meet you outside the gym door in the rear parking lot about six-thirty," she offered.

"Sounds good to me," he said. "The show starts at seven-fifteen, right?"

"Right," she confirmed.

"All right. See you then, Andi," her dad said.

She hung up the phone. It was still odd to have to plan on meeting her own dad instead of having him take her. She sighed. But that's the way things were.

"Andi?" her mom called from the top of the stairs. "Mrs. Taylor is coming over at six o'clock to stay with Timmy. So I'll drop you off, come back here, and then go back to the school for the performance. All right?"

"Sure, Mom," Andrea called back. They had agreed that it would be best to leave Timmy at home. He might get overstimulated and disrupt the performance. Andrea was glad. She didn't want to draw attention to him in light of what happened last month.

By five o'clock, Andrea finished packing her duffle bag and was ready to go. They picked up Terri on the way and arrived at the gym a few minutes early.

"See you soon," her mom called as she dropped them off.

Andrea took a deep breath and walked inside the gym. Kids were already running around backstage, attending to the sets, lighting, and sound. *This is it!* Andrea thought. *Opening night!*

"Andrea!" Ms. Vesper called. "Go into the locker room and let Terri do your makeup. Then meet me out here so we can do some voice warm-ups."

"Sure," Andrea said. The two girls went into the locker room, and Terri went to work applying heavy theatrical makeup and fixing Andrea's hair in a 1950s' style. Then Andrea put on her costume for the first act, a 1950s' outfit consisting of a full skirt with crinolines, a white short-sleeved blouse, saddle oxfords, and bobby socks.

"I look like a nerd," Andrea giggled at her reflection in the locker room mirror.

"But a cute nerd," Terri added.

Andrea walked out onto the bustling stage and over to the piano. Ms. Vesper and Tony were waiting for her. Andrea smiled broadly. Tony looked like the perfect Danny in his black T-shirt with the rolled-up sleeves, jeans, and his black leather jacket slung over his shoulder. His hair was greased back into the popular 1950s' style.

"You two look perfect!" Ms. Vesper said, beaming. "Now let's limber up those voices." She accompanied them on the piano as they concentrated on voice exercises for a few minutes.

Once they finished, Andrea asked, "What time is it?"

"Six-thirty," Tony told her.

"I need to go outside for a minute," she said. He followed her out into the cool April evening. The sun was beginning to set, and red streaks stretched across the sky. The lights in the parking lot began to flicker on.

Andrea glanced toward a couple walking toward them and recognized her dad calling to her. He came up, took her hands in his, and squeezed them. "Don't you look pretty!" he said. With a sinking feeling, Andrea watched as Jill hurried to them and leaned over her dad's shoulder.

"How adorable!" Jill cried in her high-pitched voice. Andrea smiled weakly at her. The woman's blond hair was frizzed, her dress seemed too tight, and her lipstick was too bright.

Andrea noticed someone else coming around the corner of the building. Andrea's mom spotted Andrea and began talking as she came up to the group. "There you are, Andi! I was hoping to see you before the show." Mrs. Manetti's smile quickly faded as she came up to the group and saw who all was there.

"Mom!" Andrea cried, taking her mother's hand. "I'm so glad you're here!" Andrea felt sorry for her mother. She wished she could have saved her from this meeting. Her mom and dad cautiously eyed each other.

"You look nice, Beth," her dad said with a gentleness and sincerity that Andrea hadn't heard him use since the divorce.

Andrea agreed with her dad. Her mother looked slim and poised in one of her new outfits. Her makeup and hair softened her features, too.

"Thanks, Jim," she said, cracking a smile at him. "I'm so glad you came."

"I wouldn't have missed it," he said. "We sure have a very special girl," he added. Both parents looked proudly at Andrea. She smiled and blushed. She quickly remembered that Jill and Tony were standing there, too.

"Mom, Dad, I want you to meet Tony," Andrea said. "He plays the male lead."

Andrea's dad introduced Jill, and once everyone said a self-conscious "good-bye," "good luck," and "see you after the show," her mom, dad, and Jill left, leaving Andrea and Tony alone beside the gym door in the darkening evening. Suddenly, Andrea felt sad.

"You have nice folks," Tony offered softly.

"They're divorced," she said. It was a stupid thing to say. Of course, Tony already knew that. "I wish they weren't," she added wistfully. "I miss having a family."

"You still have a family," Tony said.

"We don't even live together," she said shyly.

"So?" he said with a shrug. "At least your old man doesn't slap your mom around. And you don't have to worry that he might come after you . . . ," his voice trailed.

Andrea realized that Tony had just told her something very private about himself. She chose her words with care. "You're right. Everybody loves me. At least that's what they're always telling me."

"It's not so bad, you know," he said, "having folks who really love you. Even if they don't love each other, you know they want you."

"Well, when I get married, it's going to be forever!" she said fiercely.

Tony chuckled. "Me, too," he said.

They looked at one another for a long minute. "We'd better go back inside," he said, "before Ms. Vesper thinks we ran out on her."

Tony was right. They had a show to do!

Andrea felt that so much had happened to her since school started last September. So much had changed in her life. It was true that her mom and dad were divorced. But seeing them together tonight before the play, she realized something.

Her parents were two different and distinct people. They had new lives apart from one another. But they did love her and Timmy. She believed that with all her heart.

Tony grabbed Andrea's hand, and they looked at each other for a moment. Andrea took a deep breath. Then she and Tony quickly went back inside the gym.

ABOUT THE AUTHOR

LURLENE McDANIEL lives in Chattanooga, Tennessee, and is a favorite author of young people all over the world. Her best-selling books about kids overcoming problems such as cancer, diabetes, and the death of a parent or sibling draw a wide response from her readers. Lurlene says that the best compliment she can receive is having a reader tell her, "Your story was so interesting that I couldn't put it down!" To Lurlene, the most important thing is writing an uplifting story that helps the reader look at life from a different perspective.

Six Months to Live, the first of the four-book series about cancer survivor Dawn Rochelle, was placed in a time capsule at the Library of Congress in Washington, D.C. The capsule is scheduled to be opened in the year 2089.

Other Darby Creek Publishing books by Lurlene McDaniel include:

- *Six Months to Live*
- *I Want to Live*
- *No Time to Cry*
- *So Much to Live For*
- *My Secret Boyfriend*
- *A Horse for Mandy*
- *If I Should Die Before I Wake*
- *Why Did She Have to Die?*
- *Mother, Please Don't Die*
- *Last Dance*